NO TIME TO WAIT

"You know," Lacey said with a long sigh, "there's so many things we could have so much fun doing together."

"You think so?"

She nodded.

"Like what?" James asked. "I mean—like when?"

"That's the problem," Lacey said. "They fixed it so we wouldn't have any time."

"That's why we need a plan," said James.

"You're right. It's a war."

"Us against them. But we're losing," said James. "It's only a matter of time before Paris falls."

Lacey turned to him; her eyes were almost fierce.

"We're not prisoners *yet*," she said. "Whatever time we have left, we've gotta do what *we* want. Not what *they* want. It's our lives. And we're gonna live!"

JAMES AT 15
a 20th Century-Fox Production, for NBC Television

Starring

> LANCE KERWIN
>
> LINDEN CHILES
>
> LYNN CARLIN

Also Starring

> KIM RICHARDS

With

> DEIRDRE BERTHRONG as Kathy

Guest Star

> MELISSA SUE ANDERSON

A Special Appearance by

> VINCENT VAN PATTEN

Special Guest Star

> KATE JACKSON

Director of Photography

> CHARLES F. WHEELER, A.S.C.

Produced by

> MARTIN MANULIS

Written by

> DAN WAKEFIELD

Directed by

> JOSEPH HARDY

APRIL SMITH has published fiction and journalism in *The Atlantic Monthly, Mademoiselle,* and *Rolling Stone.*

DAN WAKEFIELD is the author of the best-selling novels *Going All the Way, Starting Over,* and most recently, *Home Free.*

James at 15

APRIL SMITH

Adapted from a screenplay by

DAN WAKEFIELD

A DELL ORIGINAL
DELL/SEYMOUR LAWRENCE

A Seymour Lawrence Book
Published by
Dell Publishing Co., Inc.
1 Dag Hammarskjold Plaza
New York, New York 10017

Dell ® TM 681510, Dell Publishing Co., Inc.

ISBN: 0-440-14389-6

Printed in the United States of America
First printing—September 1977

TO DAVID SONTAG,
GODFATHER OF "JAMES."

PART ONE

1.

James Hunter awoke that morning with a plan.

He had been watching the beautiful blonde girl in his Modern History class since the first week of school. He'd seen guys ask her out and seen her turn them down. He knew there had to be a special way to approach her and he had decided to wait until he was sure he had found it. The answer had come to him overnight, almost with the change to autumn yellow in the leaves of the maple tree outside his window. Now he was sure he would win her. He threw off the covers and swung out of bed.

His sister Sandy was knocking at his door.

"Hey, wake up," she shouted. "You'll miss the race."

"What race?" James called. Sandy was twelve and a little prankster.

"The *human* race!" she said, "Ha ha."

He threw his shoe at the door to show he thought she was a total nerd and now he couldn't find it.

Disco music was blaring from the radio as James hopped on one foot and dropped down to look under the bed. His straight blonde hair fell into his eyes. No matter what he did (once he even tried styling it with a fancy hairdryer), his hair fell unevenly, like a farm kid's, separating so that a little crescent of ear showed. He hated that. When his ear showed.

He found the shoe under a pile of clothes on the floor and jammed his foot into it, smashing the heel in a way that would make his mother mad, while he pulled a flannel shirt from the dresser.

The scent of the Oregon fall came through the open window. They had a good swimming team this year; it would be a good season. And today he felt what he did at the start of a race—anticipation. He knew he had the plan that would lead him to the greatest victory of all: Lacey Stevens finally falling in love with him.

He puffed up his cheeks and rolled his eyes at the mirror. It was the "Beaver Face" he and his friend Richie pulled at each other as a kind of signal between them during class and when they passed in the hall, meaning "This place is ab-*surd!*"

He headed for the door and swept past the Farrah Fawcett-Majors poster which said "I LUV YOU!" (caption courtesy of Richie) without bothering to turn off the radio. In the hall he smelled coffee from downstairs and heard the drone of a serious all-news radio station his parents listened to during breakfast, which he considered a total drag.

He was still buttoning his shirt as he pushed open the door of his darkroom, ignoring the sign that said "CAUTION: RADIOACTIVITY." He plunged into the dark inner sanctuary reserved for the study and adoration of his love.

Curling glossy photographs of Lacey Stevens were

fastened with clothespins to a line stretched beneath the orange darkroom light. He had been photographing her secretly, hiding behind ice cream trucks or in the bushes when she came out of school, just so he could be surrounded by her image in this dark quiet room.

But now he had another purpose. "She wants to be a model," he had overheard Lacey's girlfriend saying yesterday, "She wants to be in magazines." "She could," another girl had said, "She's cute enough." Cute enough? She was lovely, with long shiny blonde hair, and a clear delicate face. If she wanted to be a model, he would make her one. He would take beautiful photographs and present them to her. He would tell her that he'd known all along, that he could see with his photographer's eye that she was special. Together they could be rich and famous. She would see that he was serious, and she'd give herself to him in love. That was the plan. He sighed. Somewhere on the table was his Modern History notebook. He sifted through the debris—cartridges of film, empty soda bottles—and found a silver flask of "Man O Man" cologne. He pulled off the top, poured some on his hands, and slapped them against his smooth beardless cheeks. The room filled with the aroma of spice.

He found the notebook, grabbed his green canvas camera bag, and closed the darkroom door behind him. He didn't want anybody going in there.

Downstairs the Hunter family was gathered at breakfast. James's father was thumbing through a paperback textbook, peering through his glasses, as he took quick sips of coffee from a mug.

"What's the matter, Dad?" asked James. "Not prepared for class?"

"As a matter of fact, no." answered his father, who taught English Literature at the University.

James shook his head in mock disapproval.

"*I* always do *my* homework," he said, setting his gear down on the table.

"You do not," said Sandy. She wore her hair in two long braids that almost fell into the huge plate of bacon and eggs she was eating. She was trying out for the football team and said she had to eat like an athlete. She also dressed like one, in sweatshirts and jeans.

"Cereal, eggs, and juice?" asked his mother, turning from the stove. This morning she wore a dress and stockings and heels. She was going door-to-door to solicit School Committee votes.

"None of the above, thanks," said James, crossing to the refrigerator and taking out a container of milk.

"You can't go to school on an empty stomach," said his mother.

"I'm not," said James. "Look. Glass of milk."

"At least sit down at the table so we can pretend to be a civilized family," said his father.

James sat down on the edge of a chair, gulping the milk.

"Aren't you early?" asked his mother. "What's the rush?"

"Can't you tell by the *smell*?" Sandy said.

James's father took off his glasses and sniffed the air as James shot Sandy a dirty look.

"What is it?" he asked, as the spicy scent of "Man O Man" cologne drifted across the breakfast table. "Some kind of chemistry experiment?"

"Some kind of perfume for boys to make girls like them," Sandy said.

James put down his empty glass and jumped up from the table.

"*You're* going to miss the race," he told her, scooping up his gear and heading for the door. "With two broken legs."

"Ha ha," she said.

2.

James kicked through a pile of fragrant leaves at the corner of Lake Street. His camera hung around his neck.

"Hey, Ace!" It was Herman, leaning out of the white van with "HERMAN'S SUPER-ETTE" printed in big letters on the side.

"Hiya, Herm," said James. "You need me Saturday?"

"Sure do," said Herman. "Tote them bags, James." He drove the van slowly, alongside James as he walked.

"Hey," said Herman with a big wide grin. "Take my picture."

"Can't," James shrugged. "No film."

"Okay, next time." Herman waved and drove off down the street.

It was a lie, of course. He was saving the film for Lacey. In fact he had to hurry to get to his secret observation post before she got to school.

Most of the houses along this street, like the Hunter family's, were two-story weathered clapboard, big and comfortable, with wide lawns and gardens nourished by the frequent Oregon rains. The town had been built seventy years ago by people who came to work the forests and the salmon run in the nearby Chinapwa River—people who had expected to live there for some time.

You had to drive eleven miles to the Valley Shopping Center to find supermarkets, department stores, and fast-food chains. And even then the peaks of the rugged Cascade Range, visible on most days even through the fog, would remind you that the heritage of this part of the country came from the land.

James began to jog down the street, holding the camera so it wouldn't bang on his chest. The sun flashed off his hair and plaid shirt in the dappled shadows beneath maples and red-leafed oaks.

Most of his friends would work at the salmon cannery when they graduated high school, or maybe get jobs at a logging camp. They'd marry and settle close to where they grew up—not in the big old houses along Lake and Third, but in the newer apartments and condominiums in the Valley near the big papermill.

James figured he'd go to college when he graduated, but he really didn't have to think about it yet. To his embarrassment when it came to impressing Lacey, he was only a sophomore, with two years left to go.

When he came to the school he ducked around the back entrance to behind a certain bush, caught his breath, and waited.

Lacey came around the corner, talking with her girlfriend Penny. James poked the camera between the leaves, zoomed out, and focused. Her long blonde hair was blowing across her face. James watched through the lens. She was wearing a little jacket with a hood like a sweatshirt, over a flowered blouse and tight jeans. He waited for her to move out of the shadows, focusing holding his breath, now if she would only turn her head . . .

"No spies allowed on government property!" a Chinese voice hissed in his ear. A hand appeared over the lens, blocking it completely.

"Richie, ya nerd, what're ya doing?" James groaned as Richie tried to wrestle the camera away from him, knocking them both down on the grass.

"Catching spy in act!". Richie mocked in his ridiculous "Oriental Spy" voice. He was taller than James, with gangly arms and blemished skin, and he could easily pin him to the ground.

James lay there, looking up at his friend. He had almost gotten a perfect shot before Richie's attack. "Thanks a lot," he said.

"Now spy must meet fate worse than death," Richie continued, letting him up. "Must attend Miss Moger's Modern History class."

James brushed the twigs from his shirt and began to walk casually to class, turning once to belt Richie in the arm, then giving him the "Beaver Face" before running up the steps.

Actually, since he'd fallen in love with Lacey, Modern History had a whole new meaning.

She sat in front of him, a few rows to the right, where he could watch her all period long. He could watch her twirl her hair around her fingers, doodle in her notebook, lean her head on her hand and daydream, steal looks at a fashion magazine, pass notes to some gawky girl in the front row.

He imagined one day he would pass her a photo of herself looking beautiful, and she would read the note on the back that said "More to come" and turn to him with pleasure and surprise, at which point he would send her a solemn wink.

"All right, class, why was World War II the greatest war in our nation's history?" Miss Moger asked. She was standing in front of the room, a middle-aged woman who wore pantsuits and glasses and tried to make history dramatic.

"Because it had the most people in it?" Richie called.

James hardly heard his friend's reply. He was drawing a picture of Lacey in his notebook—a tiny sketch, just inside two blue-ruled lines. He was trying to capture her profile, the tilt of her nose and her bangs . . .

"No, Richard Gammons, World War II was great because of the great men who fought in it. Eisenhower. Patton." With each name Miss Moger took a step forward, like an army menacing a continent. "Nimitz. MacArthur. James Hunter?"

James sat bolt upright, his face flushing at the mention of his name. He had no idea what the teacher wanted of him and was relieved when she repeated the question.

"What were the immortal words, James, spoken by General MacArthur when the enemy drove him from the Philippines?"

James swallowed.

"I'll be back?" he guessed.

The class giggled. Lacey Stevens turned around and looked at him. Was it his imagination, or was she looking at him with sympathy and understanding in her eyes?

Miss Moger shut her eyes tightly for emphasis and unsheathed an imaginary sword.

"He said *'I shall return!'* " she declared, popping her eyes open and thrusting the sword at the ceiling.

3.

Lacey was standing on the corner by the side entrance when James and Richie came out of school that afternoon. She was holding her books and looking off down the street. She was waiting for someone and she looked different—her hair was swept off her face and held by two neat barrettes.

James slowed down. Maybe that look he'd caught in Modern History was for real. Maybe she was standing there intentionally, waiting for him to make the first move.

"Ah ha!" Richie proclaimed in his Chinese voice, "Soldier sight enemy!"

They were on their way to swimming practice, carrying their gear in duffel bags.

"They wouldn't have let you be a spy in World War II," Richie said, walking on. "Too chicken to talk to a girl."

"Oh yeah?" said James.

"Come on," Richie said, moving off toward the gym. "Let's go."

"Just a second," said James. "Hold this."

He handed Richie his duffel and carefully arranged his hair so his ear didn't show. Richie's eyes rolled toward the sky with impatience as he stood holding both duffel bags. James put his hands in his pockets and sauntered over to Lacey, who was now leaning on a car hood, still staring down the street. Only once did he look back at Richie, flashing him a wide fake grin of confidence.

"What's your favorite World War?" he asked Lacey when he was close enough to smell her cologne. Or was it his cologne?

She turned to him, surprised. "Oh, hi, James."

"Hi," he said, grinning so hard his dimples showed.

Before he could continue his dazzling repartee, a yellow Triumph sports car came screeching up to the curb. Lacey turned around to look and all of a sudden she had slipped off the car hood and was doing a little dance of excitement in the gutter, waiting for the door to open. She was smiling and her cheeks were flushed.

The car was low and sleek, and so shiny you could see the shapes of trees reflected on the sides, and James and Lacey, tiny and distorted, in the chrome hubcaps.

"Hiya, Lace. Hop on in."

It was Tony Wheeler, the infamous senior, who had shingle-cut hair down to his shoulders and wore a thin gold chain around his neck. He wore European-styled jackets to school and shirts that were always open at the throat. He leaned across to open the door for Lacey, his eyes squinting against the smoke from a cigarette which dangled carelessly from his thin lips.

"Hi, Tony," Lacey said, putting one leg in the car. "Bye, James." And she slammed the yellow door.

The car screeched off, honking its horn so the crowd of kids crossing the street would separate and let them through. Lots of them recognized Tony Wheeler behind the wheel and waved. Straining to watch, James could see Lacey lay her head on Tony Wheeler's husky shoulder as the car went off down the street.

On the next turn it would pass through the school gates and that's where James imagined the car would suddenly swerve, spin off the road, and smash into a tree where it burst into flames. He saw himself the first one on the scene, lifting Lacey from the wreckage and carrying her limp form to the grass where he'd carefully lay her down.

"Fortunately," said a newscaster voice inside James's head, "the ever-ready James Hunter was at the scene of the catastrophe. In his usual manner of cool efficiency and quiet valor, he acted with all deliberate terrific-ness."

James saw himself in that smoky scene, kneeling down beside the beautiful and unconscious Lacey. A crowd was just beginning to form. He could see the vein beating in her delicate neck, and the flicker of her eyelashes as her body sought to be awakened..

"Artificial respiration was the only answer," said the newscaster.

And James saw himself bending down to touch his warm lips to hers, forcing her mouth open slightly so he could breathe life back into her young body. In a moment she would revive, eyes fluttering until she focused on James's face, inches away from her own. She'd throw her arms around his neck.

"Oh James, you saved my life!" she would cry, burying her head in his shoulder.

"*It was nothing, really.*"

"*What about poor Tony?*"

James would pause and grow very serious as he had to tell her the truth. "*He never had a chance,*" *he would say, as gently as he could.*

"Hey!"

James snapped out of his fantasy. He had been staring at the empty road.

"Come on, man," Richie said, handing him the duffel. "We're gonna be late."

Most of the students had dispersed as Richie and James hurried down the path to the swimming pool.

"Don't let it get you down," Richie said. "They only like older guys."

"Who?"

"Sophomore girls."

"But we're as old as they are," said James, as they ran up the steps of the pool building.

"We're not *older*," Richie explained.

"Well, we will be."

"But then they will be too, see? We can't catch up. We'll never get 'em."

"Wanna bet?" said James as he pulled the door open and jogged down the hall. His face was set with determination; there had to be a way to catch up.

4.

Maybe that's why he swam so well that afternoon. Because he was determined.

He took his place at the starting mark next to Richie, feeling the anticipation tight in his belly. Beside the others he looked skinny; his chest and lips were slightly blue from the cold. The lemon lines that marked the racing lanes floated quietly on the still green water of the pool. James set his eyes on the other end. He was going to dive so far he would cover half a length.

The gun went off. Four swimmers hit the water. James was running second but looking strong. He had his rhythm. All he saw was the green and then the flashing tiled wall of the pool as he came in for a flip turn.

"Move you herd of turtles!" yelled the Coach, "Move! Richie, get the lead out! James, hit it hard! You, lane four, get some kick into it. . . ."

To James the Coach's directions were just a blur of

sound as he turned his head for air. He was pulling hard, seeing the bubbly tracks of the other swimmers, hearing the newscaster's voice in his head: "*Look at that kid James Hunter move! He is now pulling ahead of the great Japanese champ Yamamoto, formerly of World War II . . . Sweeping past the Russian Communist free-style double agent . . . This Hunter kid is some sensation!*"

Then he slapped his hand at the edge of the pool at the finish. The Coach was kneeling down, waiting for him with the stopwatch.

"Not bad, James," he said.

James spoke breathlessly, hanging in the water below him. "Good enough . . . for the meet?"

"You're in the relay," said the Coach.

James turned to see Richie gliding up to the Finish, a full ten seconds behind him.

"Congratulations, nerd," Richie gulped. His eyes were red from the chlorine and his hair was plastered over his face.

"It's only the first meet," James consoled him. "You'll make the next one."

Richie crashed over the lemon line and tried to jump on top of James to sink him like a submarine, shouting, "Dive! Dive!" as James, bobbing up to the surface and shaking his head to throw the water out of his hair, tried to do the same to his friend.

"Sure must feel great to be going to swim in the relay in the first meet of the season, huh, James Hunter?" Richie was saying as they sat at lunch in the cafeteria the next day.

Richie and James happened to be speaking in very

loud voices, not because of the cacophony of the sophomore class having lunch, but because Lacey Stevens
happened to be sitting two seats away.

The school cafeteria seemed to have been designed
as an afterthought. They put it in the basement which
had only narrow garret-like windows that let in no
light. The ceiling was low and amplified the noise,
and they used a certain disinfectant on the yellow
tiled floor whose lingering smell mixed daily with the
odor of spaghetti or weiners and sauerkraut and the
ever-present stench of sour spilled milk.

You were definitely better off if you brought your
lunch from home, as James did. He unwrapped a
creme-filled chocolate cupcake, very conscious of
Lacey's presence only two seats to his left. She was
slowly turning the pages of a fashion magazine. Two
girlfriends leaned across the table to look, saying
things like, "I *hate* that dress," "Do you think my hair
would look good that way?" James tried to get their
attention in a subtle way.

"Now that you mention it, Richie Gammons," he
said, so loudly he was practically shouting, "it *is* quite
an honor for me, James Hunter, to be swimming in . . ."

Just then everything was drowned out by the pierc-
ing squeal of feedback from the cafeteria microphone,
and everybody looked toward the front of the cafeteria to see what the announcement would be.

"Attention everybody, please. The results of the bal-
loting are in. The senior class has spoken."

The cafeteria settled down. The Officers of the senior class presided over School Council meetings and
were, in effect, officers of the entire school. Cam-
paigns had been going on all week; paper signs were
stuck on the walls, everyone wore campaign buttons,

and the entire student body had assembled in the auditorium to hear speeches which ranged from promises to jokes to one guy who just got up and played his guitar.

"The new Senior President is—Mr. Personality Himself—the Red Baron of Interstate 80—Mr. Tony Wheeler!"

Everyone in the sophomore class cheered except James and Richie who just looked at each other. Richie then stuck out his tongue and pretended to vomit. Lacey practically jumped out of her seat, clapping wildly, hair flying and eyes bright.

Tony Wheeler appeared at the front of the crowded cafeteria, loping in from nowhere to the microphone, pulling it off the stand as if he were Frank Sinatra coming on in Vegas.

He flashed the famous grin and waved his free hand at the crowd. His shirt was open three buttons down, and a silver medallion sparkled on his chest.

"There's just one word I can say, and that one word says it all." He paused. "Thanks."

The crowd went wild, whistling and cheering the new president. Lacey actually stood up and waved.

"Talk about the Gettysburg Address," Richie sneered when the place had settled down.

"That guy is really original," mocked James. "*Thanks.* That's some speech."

This time Lacey heard, all right. She leaned forward over the table so she could see around the other two girls. She had to hold her hair back with one hand so it wouldn't cover her eyes as she spoke.

"Too bad *sophomore* boys are too *juvenile* to understand anything," she said.

"*Who's* juvenile?" James demanded in a rush of anger, banging his fist down on his cupcake by mistake.

With the greatest dignity he licked the white creme-filling from his hand, stood up, pushed his chair away, picked up his books and made his way down the aisle with Richie following.

5.

The sting of despair stayed with him all afternoon and through dinner. He didn't feel like talking or doing his homework or watching TV. For an hour he just lay on his bed with the door closed, listening to music.

So much for plans. So much for big ideas. So much for anything ever turning out right. In one sentence she had completely destroyed him. Nothing else mattered. Not the swimming meet, not the test coming up in geometry, certainly not the chapter he was supposed to read for Modern History on "Rommel: The Desert Rat."

At eleven o'clock James opened the door to his room and walked quietly down the stairs. The downstairs was already dark as his parents were watching TV in their bedroom. James went down to the kitchen and silently opened the refrigerator. He found one of his father's cans of beer and timed the popping of the top to coincide with the closing of the refrigerator. Then he tiptoed back up the steps and into his darkroom, quietly closing the door behind him.

He turned on the orange safety light and looked at the latest shots of Lacey, all dried flat and stacked on the table. He had hoped to show her these. They weren't bad. He had mastered the zoom lens and caught her in action. She looked natural and the sunlight made her hair gleam. He chugged the beer, put it down half-finished, and began to tear up her pictures. Slowly, so that the torn white edges of the photographic paper showed like wounds against the grayness of the photos.

Then he heard his father's voice outside.

"Damn it, Meg, I thought you were *for* the move. I thought you were backing me on it."

James froze. His parents were passing the darkroom, heading down the steps.

"I *am* backing you," he heard his mother say. "It's just that I feel guilty about the kids." James had to press his ear to the door to hear the rest. "It's their lives too, you know."

He gave them time to go downstairs and into the kitchen, then he eased out of the darkroom like a spy, hugging the wall and sliding down the steps as he kept out of the light that now came from the kitchen.

He crept around the corner until he was just outside the kitchen door. He had brought along his can of beer.

"You agreed it would be a great opportunity for the kids," his father said.

James could hear the cabinet doors open and close and the ring of dishes being set on the table.

"I know," his mother sighed. "It's just that we're always talking to them about democracy and sharing responsibility and we didn't even let them in on the decision. We did it behind their backs."

James took a sip of beer. His heart beat faster.

"I may never get another chance like this, babe," his

father was saying in a more gentle tone. "I'm not exactly over the hill yet, but I'm past being the boy wonder of the academic world."

There was a silence. His mother sighed again.

"You're right. I know. This *is* the time to do it. And the perfect time and place for me to go back and get my Master's degree."

They were quiet. James heard the ticking of the hallway clock very close, and then the rustle of their clothes in the kitchen. Maybe they were embracing. He started to stick his head around the doorway to look, but pulled back as he heard his mother's voice.

"I'm sorry, babe," she said. The refrigerator door opened and shut. "I'm just confused and nervous. I guess it's the whole idea of going to live in a foreign city."

"Foreign?" said his father. "For Heaven's sake, we're moving to *Boston*, not *Baghdad!*"

Boston? The word rang through James's head. He clutched at his stomach, just like he did when he was clowning for Richie, but right now he wasn't clowning. He ran back up the steps to his room, suddenly not caring how much noise he made or if his parents knew that he had been listening and had heard the terrible news.

6.

As if to make up for the fact that they were uprooting their children and dragging them across the whole country to a strange city and strange new schools, James's parents took him and Sandy for a cookout on Mount Kasamoka in the national forest.

They drove up Sunday afternoon with knapsacks full of franks, rolls, homemade coleslaw and potato salad, containers of lemonade, and bags of marshmallows. It was just like a summer picnic.

But it wasn't summer any more.

At the foot of the trail they all found walking sticks and started the climb in single file, James's father in the lead. Brown and russet leaves drifted down around them as they walked and a cold breeze from further up the mountain brought the smell of pine stands and snow. The daylight that fell through the empty branches was not as brilliant as it had been in the summer, but muted, and the only sound of wildlife was the occasional cry of a crow.

His father pointed out burst seedpods and abandoned bird-nests with his walking stick, but Sandy and James didn't respond; they kept their eyes fastened on the trail. They knew this would be the last cookout of the season, and perhaps of their whole lives in Oregon.

When they came to the campsite, James and Sandy took off their knapsacks and sat down side by side on a log. Below them was a small ravine overgrown with aspen and birch with a stream that was visited by raccoon and deer—usually you could find their tracks in the mud.

"Want to climb down to the stream?" asked their mother, unpacking food.

"No thanks," said James.

"No thanks," echoed Sandy.

"Well then, make yourselves useful and get some firewood," she told them. They stood up and marched off into the woods as if they had just been sentenced to death.

When the fire was blazing, they all settled around it, holding franks on sticks over the flame.

James had rigged his stick between two rocks so he didn't have to hold it and he sat slouched down against a log with his hands in his pockets.

Sandy said in a very low voice, "I guess we won't get to go camping anymore when we move to Boston."

"Of course we'll go camping," said her father. "There's all of New England to camp in."

In response, Sandy stuck out her jaw like a gorilla.

James's parents exchanged looks.

"Now listen, gang," said his mother, running a hand through her dark hair, "moving from a small town to a big city isn't easy. But it's a wonderful *opportunity* for us. All of us. And your sister Kathy's college is only an hour from Boston, so we'll be together as a family."

"Like a modern pioneer family," his father added. "Discovering things together."

James watched a chipmunk run through the leaves behind them.

"Can't we just be a regular family?" Sandy asked.

"You ought to be glad we're not regular," said her father, "like everybody else."

"Be proud of your father," said her mother. "It's an honor to be head of the Humanities Department of a whole college."

James stared into the fire, then raised his eyes to his father. "Is it Harvard?" he asked. "Is that why it's such a big deal?"

His father took a breath and began to twirl the hot dog on the end of his stick.

"No," he said, "it's not Harvard. It's called Hastings College, and it's like Harvard only not as famous. You know, Boston is like the Super Bowl of higher education. It's a great exciting city."

Sandy flipped a braid over her shoulder.

"Home of the Red Sox," she sneered. "Never won a World Series."

"So when do we mess up our lives and move there?" asked James.

His father sighed. "Not till the end of the school year in June." he said. "We didn't want to yank you out in the middle of things. And nobody's *lives* will be messed up."

"Yeah," said James, "I bet. Hot dog."

He reached down and pulled his hot dog out of the fire, but he had left it in too long. It was black, burned, ruined.

7.

James had been watching the lady in the green pant-suit as she shopped in Herman's Super-ette, piling bottles of soda into her cart and topping it off with two ten-pound bags of kitty litter. He crossed his arms at the check-out counter and waited for his fate—to carry those grocery bags what seemed like thirteen miles to her car.

"And how are you, James?" the lady asked, smiling, as she paid her bill.

"Fine, thank you," he said without looking up as he continued to pack her groceries into big brown bags. He couldn't help it. He felt like a prisoner. A prisoner to his parents' decision to move across the country, a prisoner to this lady and her soda and kitty litter. For a few days he had felt angry and confused. But now, caught in the routine of work at the grocery store, he felt only resignation.

"I'm parked at the end of the block, James," the lady called, striding out in front of him. He struggled to scoop both bags up at the same time and walked sideways out the door. He could hardly see over the celery and bread that lay at the very top of the bags.

He tried to keep the green lady in sight, but instead he saw Lacey, who was walking down the street in the opposite direction.

He made an abrupt about-face in the middle of the block.

"Hey, Lacey," he called.

"Hi, James," she said without stopping.

He ran to catch up with her, squeezing the grocery bags in the middle, his arms aching. He was almost at the point of dropping everything.

"Guess what?" he said, struggling alongside her. "I'm moving to Boston."

She glanced at him.

"Really?"

He nodded. His hair fell in his eyes.

"Yep. My Dad got this job as head of some college's whole Humanities Department. In Boston."

"Yo-hoo! James! I'm parked down *here!*" called the lady from the other end of the block.

James tried to ignore her.

"It's a long way," he told Lacey breathlessly. "You'll probably never see me again."

They had reached the corner.

"Well, it ought to be an interesting experience," Lacey said, blinking her eyes and looking down the block. She shifted the denim bag on her shoulder. "Good luck, James," she said, and crossed the street.

James stared after her, still clutching the grocery bags. Then he wiggled his hips in imitation of big-shot Tony Wheeler and said, "There's only one word I can say and that says it all. *Thanks!*"

"*James!*" called the lady. "Are you trying to steal my groceries?"

* * *

James and his father were playing one-on-one in the driveway of their house, shooting for a weathered hoop which was mounted over the garage door. The white paint around the hoop was blackened by many seasons of father-and-son basketball. James's father looked younger in a T-shirt and jeans, although his thick hair was prematurely gray. His body was still in good shape from playing rugby in college and squash with colleagues at his school.

"Do you believe in love at first sight?" James asked his father.

"Well that's how it was when I first met your mother," he replied, going in for a lay-up shot. "I mean, it was that way for me. For her it took longer."

"How long?"

"Till we got to college. Couple of years, I guess." He tossed the ball at James, who caught it at his stomach and stood stock-still.

"*Years?*" he asked.

"Most worthwhile things take time," said his father, rushing at him to force a shot. "You have to get to know a person, the way they are, the way the two of you are together."

"How can you tell?" asked James.

"There aren't any rules." His father stopped playing to tell him a story. "You know, your mother turned me down the first time."

"She did?"

"I'll never forget it. At a big formal sorority dance. I asked her to wear my fraternity pin, which was a sign of pledging eternal love back then, and she turned me down."

"Really?"

He nodded. "It was when we were dancing a slow

romantic number, cheek to cheek. She told me no, and suddenly I let out the loudest belch of my life."

James giggled.

"I guess I was nervous. She looked at me in horror and I panicked. But then I was inspired. I put my right hand over my chest and said, 'Be still, sad heart.' And you know what she did?"

"Belched?"

"No. She laughed, thank God."

"So you knew it was okay," said James, starting to bounce the ball. "You knew she liked you."

"Sure." His father put his arm around James's shoulder as they walked toward the house. "Try to hang loose, James," he said. "See some other girls. Play the game for a while."

8.

He had to get Lacey off his mind.

In the bottom of an old Monopoly set, he kept a stash of *Playboy* magazines which he had stolen from the next-door neighbor's trash. He locked the darkroom from the inside, opened the box and took out the false cardboard bottom where you were supposed to keep all the little pieces for the game, and removed three well-worn copies of the glossy magazine.

He turned on the safety light and spread his sleeping bag on the floor. He lay down on his stomach. The color photographs looked especially enticing in the dim orange light. As he turned the pages, images of women with bright red lips, in all sorts of erotic settings—on fur, with feathers, carrying fans and animals—rose and fell before him. He opened to the centerfold and stared at *Playboy's* version of perfection. He wasn't thinking of Lacey any more. The sensual details of the model on the page captured his imagination. He could feel the soft folds of the sleeping bag beneath him, and the hard floor beyond.

And then his mother knocked on the door.

"James? May I come in? I'd like to discuss a project."

He jumped up as if someone had snuck up behind him and jabbed him in the spine.

"Ah—yeah," he said. "Just a sec."

He kicked away the sleeping bag, hid the *Playboys* back in the Monopoly box and touched his hair so his ear didn't show. His hand was shaking as he unlocked the door.

"Were you busy?" asked his mother, glancing at the general mess in the small room.

"Oh, no," said James, standing with his hands in his back pockets. "Just going to have a little game of Monopoly."

"By yourself?"

"Well . . . yeah," he said, tossing his head to get the hair out of his eyes, "there's a kind of—solitaire version you can play."

As he stood before her he was certain she knew he was lying so he flashed her a wide fake grin.

"Well, what I wanted to talk to you about is this outdoor sports-fest at the Treadway Farm on Sunday. I'm taking over some food and I thought you and Richie might like to come."

"Oh." James felt the old wave of sadness come over him again for no reason at all. "Thanks." He sat down. "But I don't feel much like doing anything."

His mother watched him thoughtfully. "You know when's the best time to do things, James?"

"When?"

"When you don't feel like doing anything. I know," she said, "Don't you think there're times I feel like staying in bed with the covers over my head? Days I don't want to think about how you and Sandy and

Dad'll get dinner, or whether the day care volunteers will get picked up, or if Elaine White needs my vote for School Committee? When you feel like that, you've got to make yourself get out and do something."

"Like what?"

"Swim, maybe. Run. Get out your camera again. Take some pictures."

"Of what?" James asked mournfully. He was never going to take pictures of Lacey Stevens again.

"I don't know. Something you like. Something that's important to you. Something fun."

James nodded. His mother touched him sympathetically on the head. She left the room, leaving the door open. It was no use. He couldn't hide or just lie around and hope the sadness would go away. He'd have to do something.

9.

"I'm looking for *action*," said Mr. Harper. "You got any action shots?"

James stood in front of Mr. Harper's big oak desk in the office of *The Express*, the town's newspaper.

"I think so." James shuffled through his camera bag for some other prints.

Mr. Harper, the city editor, was a friend of James's father. He said he'd look at James's photos to see if he could use him to cover high school sports. James had photographed sports events for the high school paper, and he showed Mr. Harper some shots of basketball players going up for the jump.

"Not bad," said the editor. "But do you have anything with feeling? Something that tells a story. *Says* something about the subject. And no more cats. I've seen enough portraits of cats to last a lifetime."

At the bottom of the pile was the last photograph James had taken of Lacey. It was the only one he hadn't ripped up. It showed her walking with Penny near the school. You could see by the way they were talking they were good friends.

"Now that tells a story," said the editor, snuffing out a cigarette. "Right?"

James nodded. He didn't really like to look at that photograph any more.

"Okay, kid," said Mr. Harper, pushing away from his desk. "Cover the football game on Saturday. I want *action*. But I also want *people*. Got it?"

The noise of the band was deafening as James crouched down in front of the leader on the sidelines of the field. It was the first game of the season and the bleachers were packed with kids and their parents and people from town.

James had strapped just about every piece of camera equipment he owned to his body, with the camera bag hanging from his shoulder to hold lenses and film. A yellow card tied with a string around a button of his jacket said "PRESS." It was given to James by the editor.

"Now hit the streets and get that story," he heard Mr. Harper saying in his head. It was 3:00 A.M. and the newsroom was deserted. "Great Caesar's Ghost! You're the only one who can cover it."

"Right, Chief," said Ace Photographer James Hunter. "I'll get the scoop, all right. I'll catch the spies in the act of trading government documents."

"Just be careful," Mr. Harper warned. He wore a green eyeshade and rolled-up sleeves. "Remember, you're on your own."

"I know, Chief," said James, snuffing out his own cigarette and shouldering his camera bag. "But this story might change history."

"If you're caught," said the editor, *"I'll have to pretend we never had this conversation."*

"I understand."

"And James . . ."

"Yes, Chief?"

Mr. Harper's face was haggard under the hanging yellow light bulb. He spoke softly and meaningfully. *"We're holding the front page for you,"* he said.

The shrill whistle of the kickoff brought James back to reality. He kneeled in the grass and focused with the zoom lens. He began to concentrate, the noise of the band and the cheering of the crowd fading away. He was watching the halfback, Rip Lindeman, through the lens. Lindeman was a talented ballplayer, the best on the team. James watched the way he moved, following him with the camera, and in the second quarter he started taking pictures. Tell a story. Show a person in action. . . .

Sandy usually hated delivering papers on Sunday because the edition was so heavy and thick, but the next morning at 7:30 A.M. she rode her bike along her paper route shouting, "Extra! Extra! Read all about it! Hunter makes front page!"

And there it was. A photograph by her brother on the front page of the Sunday paper.

The headline read "LINDEMAN RIPS BULL-DOGS" and underneath the picture of the halfback in action was the line *Photo Credit: James Hunter.*

James happened to be wearing his camera in school all day Monday.

"Hey, Front Page Hunter!" called a boy James didn't even know. "Nice going."

James smiled at the kid and gave him a wave. He was standing by his locker, getting his stuff ready for the swim meet that afternoon. A clip of the photo was taped to the inside of his locker door. He looked at it again. *Photo Credit: James Hunter.* And then, in the locker mirror, he saw the chest of Rip Lindeman himself.

"You the guy who took the shot?" Rip asked, nodding toward the photo on the door.

James looked up at the star halfback. Lindeman's neck was as thick as James's thigh. His hand, wrapped around his notebooks, looked big as James's head. His shoulders were immense. He wore an athletic terry cloth headband around his long straight hair and a maroon sweater with the high school letter and his name embroidered over the pocket in script: "Rip."

"Who, me?" asked James. "In the paper? Oh. Yeah."

The other kids who were standing around their lockers grew quiet, and watched James talking with Rip.

"That was some kinda shot," said Rip, punching James so his arm-bone hurt. "I mean de-cent. Real de-cent."

James flushed. "Hey, thanks," he said. "Great game you had."

Rip shrugged. Some girls were behind him, staring.

"Couldn't lose against those turkeys," said Rip, maybe sensing the audience. "Listen, you got some more shots? I'll buy a few off ya."

"Nah," said James, imitating the rough way Rip talked, "I'll make 'em up for ya free."

Rip nodded solemnly. James was now on the team.

"Class, buddy, real class," he said, holding out his hand, palm up.

James stared at the palm. It could crush his face in an instant. Was he supposed to put something in it? Like the photos? Or money? Then he remembered— the pro football shake on TV. With a smile of relief, James brought his own palm down with a solid slap on Rip's. The kids around them almost gasped out loud.

Rip turned and sauntered off down the hall. James went back to his locker, whistling, as if nothing very unusual had happened.

He slammed the locker shut and gave the combination lock a casual spin. Turning down the hall, he almost walked into Lacey Stevens, who happened to have been one of the girls who had been standing behind Rip.

"James," she said, actually smiling at him, "I didn't know you were such a good photographer."

"Yeah, well," he said, "thanks, Lace. Gotta rush. Swimming meet," and he strode off down the hall, feeling light-headed and high.

"Hey, James," called Richie, running to catch up with him, "was that Rip Lindeman you were talking to?"

"Who'd it look like?" James replied, "Amy Carter?"

"Was that Lacey Stevens back there, the one you hurried right past?"

"You don't miss a thing, Rich."

"So what's going on? You some kinda stud all of a sudden?"

James spoke with a Chinese accent. "Just old friend spy, now in clever new disguise." Then he gave Richie the "Beaver Face," much to the astonishment of a passing science teacher.

* * *

The clever new disguise was working, because Lacey was at the swim meet that afternoon. Not many people attended the meets, but she was sitting in the middle of the stands, watching James and cheering him on.

James imagined himself riding in the back of an open car as crowds cheered. He was wearing a General MacArthur-style hat with braid, dark glasses, leather jacket, and clenching a corncob pipe between his teeth as he waved to the adoring multitudes . . .

When he pulled himself from the pool after the relay she was waiting for him. He had thrown a towel around his shoulders and was dripping water all over the floor. The team had won.

"That was really something, James," Lacey said.

He shrugged, dripping water on her shoe and poking his ear with a corner of the towel.

"Nah," he said, "that was nothing. But thanks." He gave her a wave and pushed through the swinging door to the locker room.

When he returned home that evening his hair was still wet from the meet, and his face was flushed from the joyous run home. He had taken action. Victory was his. He burst into the living room to find his family sprawled around their favorite places. Mom was writing at a small desk, Dad was reading, Sandy was watching re-runs of *The Three Stooges* on TV.

James jumped up onto the couch, bouncing his father where he sat, and raised his right arm in the air as if he were leading an army with a sword. "I have returned!" he shouted.

"James," his mother scolded, "please get your feet off the couch."

10.

The next time James saw Tony Wheeler's car, it was screeching up to the curb just as before. The yellow door popped open and Mr. Personality Himself leaned over to welcome a pretty girl inside. But this time the girl wasn't Lacey. It was some blonde cheerleader on her way to practice. She wore a little maroon skirt and carried her pom-poms, doing a little dance of excitement as she got into Tony Wheeler's car. James watched as they drove off down the street and the cheerleader laid her head on Tony Wheeler's shoulder.

He shook his head and walked on, past the bush he used to hide behind to take pictures of Lacey. He was glad those heartsick days were over. Then he saw Lacey herself standing right by the bush.

"Hi, James," she called as he passed.

"How're you doin', Lace?"

"The pits," she said, "the absolute pits."

She walked forward and fell into step beside him. James realized she had seen Tony Wheeler drive off with the cheerleader.

"Hey, I'm sorry," he said, looking over at her walking close to him and, in spite of himself, he felt his heart melt all over.

"I'm the one who's sorry," Lacey said, keeping her eyes on the sidewalk, "for going out with an older guy who thinks he's God's Gift to the Western World. They're all that way."

"Older guys are?"

She nodded. "They all think they're Mr. Cool because they drive a car. Big deal."

"Yeah," James agreed.

"But *you're* not like that," Lacey said, suddenly lifting her eyes to him. "You're a *genuine* person."

James reached up to touch his hair. He didn't want his ear showing at a moment like this. They continued to walk and when Lacey turned down a different street, James found himself turning with her. They were walking toward Lacey's house. He couldn't believe it. He was walking her home!

"James," said Lacey, "you know, once a person like Tony Wheeler has done something like that to you, it takes time to recover."

"I know."

"And you don't see things the same way anymore, you know?"

"I know."

"So you might realize there's been somebody all along . . . who suddenly looks different. Someone who might have just been a friend could turn out to be . . . a real good friend."

James nodded. They had reached her house. It was a modern ranch-style, not like the big old houses on James's street. A flagstone path and cement steps led up to the front door. James and Lacey sat down on the steps.

She pulled her knees to her chest and wrapped her arms around them, all curled up in a ball.

"You and I could be friends," said Lacey. "Couldn't we? There's no reason why not."

"Absolutely none."

"And then, maybe in time . . ."

"A long time?" asked James.

"Who can know about these things?" Lacey said.

He remembered his father's story about the fraternity pin.

"Right," he said.

"Do you understand?" she asked slowly, shifting her eyes toward him.

"Sure. Of course."

She sat up a little and sighed.

"I knew you were an understanding-type person."

She was looking at him now with full force, straight and deep. He was lost in her eyes. She was closing them, slowly, and tilting her face up to his. And he was bending down until his lips were tenderly touching hers.

"James Hunter strikes again!" shrieked a voice from the street.

Startled, James and Lacey broke apart.

It was Sandy zooming by on her bicycle, wearing a football helmet.

"Is that a friend of yours?" Lacey asked.

"No. A sister." He stared grimly after her.

"Well, you know," said Lacey, standing up suddenly, "we have a lot in common."

He hastily got up to stand beside her. "I know," he said. And then, "But what is it?"

She bent down to pick up her books. "We're both fifteen and we're both . . . adventurous."

She waited. It was as if she knew how she looked at

that moment, with the sunset light washing the doorway with an orange glow, coloring her hair and sending warmth to her eyes. . . . As if she sensed the whirlwind building deep inside James's body, swirling and rising until he couldn't breathe, couldn't hold it in any longer, until he blurted out, "I love you!"

Then she smiled, as if that were what she had been waiting to hear. She touched his arm and drew him closer. "That's what else we have in common. I realize now that I love you, too."

And James kissed her again as they stood on the doorstep of her parents' house.

"Will you take lots of pictures of me?" she murmured.

11.

"I should have broken your arm for what you did to me and Lacey," James told his sister, "but luckily you did it yourself. Clod."

"It's not broken, it's sprained," Sandy said as they pushed her bicycle along, the sack holding *The Express* hanging from the handlebars.

"It happens in athletic competition," she told him. "The Coach says you have to work through the pain."

"Sure," said James. "That's why I have to do your paper route for you. The big hero."

He was tossing rolled copies of the paper onto people's doorsteps.

"That's the Huddlestons'," Sandy said as they passed a yellow frame house. "You don't even have to hit the porch. They're liberals."

He gave it a sidearm.

"They shouldn't have stuck me at linebacker," Sandy said. "I'm more of a middle-guard type. The brick house is Avery—they want it on the front steps." He let a paper fly. "Hey, James, what's it feel like?"

"What's what feel like?"

"Being in love."

"Who's in love?"

"Aw c'mon, James, I've seen you walking home from school with Lacey Stevens every day for the past three days. When you look at her it looks like you might be sick. Is that how it feels?"

"None of your business."

"Don't be a creep. Tell me."

"No."

James couldn't figure out how everybody knew. It seemed to have taken about twenty-four hours for everybody in the school to be talking about James-and-Lacey. They were suddenly welded together, a separate category, a "couple."

"You have to tell me," Sandy continued. "It's part of my apprenticeship as a writer. Learning how people feel in their deepest emotions. Otherwise my story's no good."

"What story?" asked James, only half-listening.

"I call it 'James in Love.' Mrs. Cranburn says if I put some more insights in it they'll print it in the literary magazine."

She stood there smiling at him from under her yellow bangs as if nothing were wrong.

"Are you kidding?" James exclaimed. "Where's the story? Give it to me."

Sandy dropped the bag of papers and ran for their house, shouting over her shoulder, "I'll change the name of it! I'll call it 'Thomas in Love.' No one'll ever know!"

James let go of the bicycle and let it fall on the sidewalk. He dashed after his sister and grabbed her around the waist just as she reached the front door. She started to giggle hysterically.

"Come on, James," she said. "Really, I'll change it. No one'll know."

"I won't let you go until you show me that story," said James, tickling her in the ribs until she was sagging, weak with laughter, then catching the laughter himself, because he didn't care if everybody knew.

12.

The House of Ming Chinese Restaurant had scarlet walls and black booths and a pair of golden dragons above the doors. It was the only ethnic restaurant in town, and it was beginning to look rather worn after twenty-five years of the responsibility of serving egg rolls and wonton soup to generations of blonde, ruddy-cheeked Oregon kids and their parents.

The Hunter family had been eating there since James was three and his mother told him if he ate up all his food he would find a blue dragon on the bottom of his plate. James still liked to find the dragon on the bottom of his plate. Or sometimes it would be a Chinese sailing ship.

"I've got some news for you," Dad announced when they had finished supper and the table was laden with aluminum serving dishes and lids and white bowls of rice crusting over in the air.

"Good or bad?" asked James, popping a last noodle in his mouth.

"Depends on your point of view."

"I'll tell you some good news," said his mother, "Kathy's coming home from college for Thanksgiving."

"Yay," Sandy cheered, trying to drum her chopsticks on the red tablecloth.

"Enough of that," said her mother, grabbing the chopsticks and making her stop.

James saw that his mother was tense. He looked back and forth between his parents.

"What's the other news?" he asked.

First his father lined up his fork and knife and chopsticks in a row beside his plate. Then he looked up at Sandy and James and folded his hands on the edge of the table. Then he unfolded his hands and rubbed the back of his head and smiled in a frank friendly way.

James knew something was wrong.

"Well, first I have to tell you that what I'm going to tell you was as big a surprise to me as it will be to you."

"Here comes the bad news." James braced himself.

"You see, the man whose position I'm taking in Boston was scheduled to retire next June," his father explained, "but he got very sick and can't come back. So instead of starting in the fall, the college needs me for the spring term." He stopped.

"The spring?" cried James. It was impossible. "You mean we'll have to leave in a couple of months?" He threw his red napkin on the table.

"Can't Daddy live in a hotel in Boston and come home weekends?" Sandy whined.

"Sandy!" Their mother looked shocked. "Boston is three thousand miles away. We're a family! We go together."

James stood up.

"Sure we have to go," he said. "We're prisoners."

"Please, James," said his father, "sit down and have dessert."

"I don't want any damn dessert." James's eyes blurred with tears of rage. "You ruined it."

"I would have started as shortstop this spring." Sandy began to sob and her face turned all hot and pink. People at the next table turned to look.

"You still can," said her father, his voice a little shaky. "Only in Boston."

"I *hate* the Red Sox!"

"Sit down, James," said his mother, "so we can discuss what this means for all of us."

James flopped into his seat with a curse.

"What if we don't choose to participate?" Sandy asked, wiping her eyes angrily with the back of her hand.

"Don't pull that fake democracy stuff on us, young lady," ordered her father. "You and your brother will sit here, and behave, and finish your dinner."

The waiter came and cleared away the dishes. James stared at the table, jaws clenched. He wouldn't do it. He'd run away. They couldn't control his life like this.

The waiter set a little dish of fortune cookies in front of them. James grabbed one and crushed it to bits in his fist. He pulled the fortune from the wreckage of crumbs and gasped as he read, "Sudden long journey means separation from Loved One."

Gongggg. An Oriental gong sounded in his head. He saw his father and mother dressed in scarlet Mandarin robes embroidered with fierce dragons. They stood on a white platform, their arms folded across their chest. His father had a long Fu Manchu moustache and his mother had dark Oriental eyes.

Beside them was a Henchman with a droopy mous-

tache, wearing a round hat and a golden silk jacket rolled up at the sleeves so his massive muscles showed as he struck the gong with a fifty-pound mallet.

Gongggg.

"Confucious say young infidels must be separated," snarled his father in Richie's Chinese accent voice..

His mother, the dragon lady, nodded. "Ah so," she said.

James and Lacey stood before them, holding hands. With a nod from his father, the Henchman ducked off the platform and grabbed Lacey, snorting through his nose like a beast. She let out a shriek.

"Don't be afraid, Lacey," James called. His parents swooped off the platform to grab him, but his sneakers were fast on the slippery red floor of the palace, as he escaped them to run after the Henchman who was dragging Lacey away.

He dealt the giant a couple of swift karate blows, took Lacey's hand and ran with her.

"They'll never separate us," he vowed.

"Finish with tea, sir?" asked a gentle Chinese waiter bending over James, who was startled out of his heroic fantasy to find himself back at the House of Ming Restaurant in Oregon.

13.

"How can they do this to us?" Lacey cried.

"They don't even care," said James, folding his legs up Indian-style. "We're just some kind of trained animals they have. Like pet cats and dogs. We've got just as much say in things as a dog."

They were sitting on the couch in the game-room of Lacey's parents' house, surrounded by books they were supposed to be studying. It was four o'clock in the afternoon, the Modern History test was the next day, and they had barely gotten through the chapter "The Seeds of War."

The room had been built as an addition to the house. The insulation was poor and they were freezing. The fireplace had not yet been used that season. On the mantelpiece were several new photos James had taken of Lacey.

She poured more Coke into a mug. They had almost gone through a quart of it, along with a big bag of yellow Dispy Doodles and a bowlful of M & M's.

"So what are we going to do?" she asked.

"I don't know," said James. "Maybe we should have a plan."

"Like what?"

"Like D-Day. Or the Marshall Plan. Or the Maginot Line. That stuff they had in World War II."

"Sometimes you don't need a plan," Lacey said. "Sometimes things just . . . happen."

She turned her head toward him and closed her eyes, then let them open, slowly. She was waiting. James put his arm around her and she laid her head against his shoulder with a sigh and stared out across the room. James moved his fingers around in a circle where he was holding her. She wore a soft wool sweater and James became lost in the feel of it, around and around, even if it was only her left arm.

Lacey sighed again and slipped down so her head rested on his thigh. He looked down at her. She was still staring peacefully across the room. He now had her whole sweater at his disposal.

He cleared his throat. His fingertips were making spirals along the light blue wool. His other hand rested like a piece of dead wood on the arm of the sofa. He didn't know what to do with it, so he just left it there and concentrated on this one, spiraling up along her shoulder and down her collar bone.

Lacey shifted her head and James stopped, afraid. But she was just nestling closer to him. His fingers continued and his breath came faster.

"I'm going out for a while, now, dear," called Lacey's mother from the other side of the closed game-room door.

James's hand flew off her daughter's chest.

But Lacey answered calmly, "Okay, Mom."

"You and James study hard now," she said.

"Don't worry, Mom, we're crackin' the old books."

She giggled up at James.

"I won't be gone *too* long," her mother said.

"We get the message, Mom." Lacey sat up, resigned. They heard her mother walk off down the hall. "They don't even give us credit for knowing when they've got us trapped."

James reached for his mug, found it empty, and poured off the last of the Coke.

"There ought to be a Liberation for Minors," Lacey said, untangling her hair with her fingers. "Like a movement. Minor Minority Rights."

James gulped down the Coke, staring at her over the mug.

"You know," she said with another long sigh, "there's so many things we could have so much fun doing together."

"You think so?"

She nodded.

"Like what?" James asked. "I mean—like when?"

"That's the problem," Lacey said. "They fixed it so we wouldn't have any time."

"That's why we need a plan," said James.

"You're right. It's a war."

"Us against them. But we're losing," said James, "It's only a matter of time before Paris falls."

Lacey turned to him; her eyes were almost fierce.

"We're not prisoners *yet*," she said. "Whatever time we have left, we've gotta do what *we* want. Not what *they* want. It's our lives. And we're gonna live!"

She threw her arms around James, crushing his lips with hers as they fell backward on the couch, wrestling to press their bodies against each other as hard as they possibly could, as if to seal the pact.

14.

Kathy came home from college for Thanksgiving and surprised them all with her new haircut. Her hair used to fall halfway down her back but now it just swept her shoulders in a smooth neat style that was almost businesslike. She wore a new pair of pressed jeans and a ski sweater over a blouse. Something had changed in her since she had gone off to college. She seemed quieter, more determined.

Kathy sat in the middle of the family portrait James was arranging at the dining room table. Before them was the feast—golden roast turkey, the Hunter family crystal filled with cranberry sauce, squash, mashed potatoes, salad, homemade buns, and steaming green beans almondine (made by Kathy), with two candles lit on either side of a basket filled with straw flowers and cattails which she had brought back from Boston.

James had assembled his tripod across from them, set the camera for a time exposure, and was running around the table as the timer clicked.

"Say cheese!" he told them, dashing to his place.

"Cheeeese!" they said as the shutter snapped and the flash went off.

"Oh boy," Sandy said. "Turkey!"

They settled into their places and began passing food. His father called for attention by tapping on the side of his water glass with a Hunter family silver knife.

"Before we stuff ourselves into oblivion," he said, "I think we should all be aware that in spite of some problems, we have a whole lot to be thankful for this year."

"At least Kathy's home," said James.

"Hey, thanks," said his sister.

"And better still," added his mother "she'll be able to come up from college and visit us all the time when we move to Boston. Gravy, anyone?"

Kathy rubbed the side of her nose. "That would be wonderful, folks," she said, not looking at anyone, "except I might not be there next year."

The passing of food momentarily stopped. Sandy's eyes remained glued to the gravy boat, which her father held in mid-air.

"You're not dropping out?" he exclaimed.

"You're not *flunking* out?" said her mother.

"You're not going to have a baby?" said Sandy.

Her father almost dropped the gravy boat. Luckily Sandy's hands were already on it.

"Will everyone hold it please?" Kathy said, putting her hands up in front of her. "I applied for this exchange program where you get to study for a year at a foreign university in an emerging nation."

Her father put down his napkin and said, "My God."

"Which emerging nation?" asked her mother with a quick look at her husband.

"My first choice is Zaire."

"Where is that emerging from?" asked James.

"Africa."

Even Sandy stopped ladling gravy over her plate. "You get to go to college in Africa?"

"Do they have a high school?" asked James.

"Maybe we could all go!" Sandy cried. "Instead of Boston!"

With that, her father pushed his chair from the table and stood up.

"Alan!" said her mother. "What are you doing?"

"Right now I'm standing up," he replied, "but my plan is to go lie down."

"You sit right back there and finish your dinner. It's still Thanksgiving."

"Yeah," said James, passing a bowl of squash, "we ought to be thankful that at least Kathy gets to do what she wants."

"James!" said Kathy. "Be thankful that whatever we do or wherever we go, we're still a *family!*"

Their father sat back down.

"Thank you for saying that, Kathy," he said.

Every Thanksgiving it had been this way, for as long as James could remember: the rich smell of a turkey roasting, the fire they kept going in the living-room, the small glasses of sherry the kids were allowed to drink before the meal. Sometimes there were more people—grandparents and cousins—but it always began with a glass of sherry and ended, as now, at eight o'clock at night, with everyone sacked out, snoring.

Kathy was alone in the kitchen, making her way slowly through a huge pile of dishes and pots. She had turned classical music on the radio, put on her mother's blue-checked apron, and seemed in no hurry to finish.

James watched her from the doorway. He could see her face reflected in the dark steamy window above the sink. It reminded him of a holiday season many years ago. . . . It was Christmas because the face he remembered was Kathy's, through a window at night, singing carols. She was with a group of high school friends (she must have been his age—fifteen), but her arm was linked with Rick Bender's as they stood outside the window and sang.

James remembered the fight she'd had with their mother that night. It was Christmas Eve, and their parents wanted her to stay home. But Rick had asked her to go caroling, and he had a car and she had a crush on him, and she cried and cried when her parents said no. Then Kathy had done an extraordinary thing. James had been in the living room waiting to finish trimming the tree when she came flying down the stairs, screaming, "It's my life and I'm old enough!" and flew out the door into the snowy night.

A few hours later they heard carolers outside and drew back the curtains of the living room to see Kathy and Rick and their friends, cheeks rosy, eyes bright, singing their hearts out to make it up to his parents.

She must have really loved Rick to run out of the house like that on Christmas Eve.

James joined her at the sink and began to hand her plates.

"Thanks, James," she said, "but I can do it."

"It's okay," he said. "Are you really going to school in Africa?"

"Not for sure," she said, "I have to get the grant first. Lots of people apply."

"Well, if you want it, I hope you get it," said James. "But I wish you'd be around, sort of."

"In general," she asked, "or because of something specific?"

She wiped a strand of hair from her eyes with the back of a blue rubber-gloved hand, dripping soap.

"I dunno," said James. "Kath—" he stopped. "Kath—when you were a girl—"

"You mean I'm not anymore?"

"I mean, when you first went out with guys and all. Like when you really liked one—"

"Yes?"

"Well. It's about me and Lacey. You know what I mean."

Kathy turned off the water. "You mean you're confused, like everyone, when this new feeling comes over you and you want everything to be perfect, right?"

"Yeah."

"Not only for you but for the other person."

"See, it's hard," said James, "because we have to come up with a plan. . . ."

"Oh," said Kathy, "You can't plan. You think there are special secrets or handbooks about it—about having a relationship—like 'Electronics Made Easy'?"

"Well, aren't there? Secrets, I mean."

"Surprise!" Kathy smiled. "There aren't. The best you can do is be natural and considerate and you'll grow together."

"Like with you and Rick?"

"Rick?"

"Rick Bender."

"Rick Bender!" Kathy laughed. "You're kidding! That was ages ago. I think he's married."

"Oh."

"The best you and Lacey can do," Kathy repeated, "is try to make it mutual."

"Mutual?"

"Whatever you do, work it out *together*. In concert."

James was holding the salad bowl. He stopped, perplexed, trying to figure it out.

"But if you don't have a car," he said at last, "*where do you have the concert?*"

15.

James and Lacey tried to have the concert—or at least an overture—in the back row of the Union Movie House, a baroque theater built sixty years ago for vaudeville. Heavy red velvet curtains framed the screen and a plaster frieze of cupids, goddesses, and other romantic figures was carved around the arched ceiling.

James and Lacey were kissing, hard, when a middle-aged couple came squeezing past them; the woman had fat legs, a swinging pocketbook, and an air of utter disapproval.

"Excuse *us*," said the woman, indignantly.

James and Lacey broke apart and slumped, discouraged, in their seats.

"If only we had a car," whispered Lacey.

"Yeah," James said, "Too bad I'm not Tony Wheeler. Then we'd have a real muscle car and could go anywhere and do anything—like you and him probably did."

"If you talk like that, I'll leave," Lacey hissed.

"I'm sorry," said James. "I'm even sorrier I can't find us a car."

Lacey took James's hand in consolation and turned her eyes back toward the screen.

"I can!" James exclaimed.

"Shhhhh!" she said. "Can what?"

"Get us a car!"

The key was already in the ignition, so they turned on the radio to a soft rock station, climbed into the back seat, and kissed in the glow of the green dashboard light.

Suddenly Lacey pulled away.

"I feel silly," she said.

"We're in a car, aren't we? We're parking, aren't we? Why's it silly?"

"Because it's your parents' car in your parents' garage and your parents are inside right this minute."

"Just pretend we're on a lonely road, parked on a wind-blown cliff, high above the sea, just outside Paris."

"I'll try," Lacey said, as James lunged at her again.

Their down-filled jackets made slippery nylon sounds as they hugged. It wasn't a very romantic setting: the air was stale and smelled of gas and they were surrounded by garden hoses and tools and, in the back, a collapsed rubber swimming pool.

Suddenly the garage was flooded with light. James and Lacey sat up.

At the door leading from the garage to the kitchen stood James's parents. Staring.

"Sandy thought she heard burglars," his father said.

"Yeah," said James through the open window of the back seat, "there were, but we scared them away."

James's mother saw her husband still staring in shock and said quickly, "You kids must be freezing. Come inside. I'll make us all some hot chocolate."

James opened the back door and he and Lacey crawled out.

"Some wind-blown cliff high above Paris," she muttered as they trudged dejectedly into the kitchen.

"Hey, James, you making first downs with old Lacey yet?" asked a kid on the swimming team in the locker room after a practice.

"First downs, nothin'," said another, "I bet he's scored."

"That right, James?" Richie asked, jumping up on the bench near him. "You made a touchdown yet?" The guys had begun to crowd around him. "C'mon, James, tell."

James was rubbing his hair dry with a towel, trying to ignore them.

"Tell us what you got. A touchdown or only a field goal?"

James threw the towel back in his locker, ran a comb through his hair, kicked the locker closed, and collected his books.

"Okay, you guys. You promise not to tell if I tell you the most I ever did with Lacey?"

"Yeah, sure!" they cried, pressing closer.

James took a deep breath. "A lateral reverse fake pass from a wishbone-T formation with the flankers wide and a flare from the strong-side line."

The guys looked at each other in confusion as James said, "Excuse me," and broke through the circle toward the door.

"A *what?*" called Richie.

"Oh, yeah," said James, turning back, "and a side of coleslaw."

There was a pause and then a rain of objects thrown at James.

"You double-crossing nerd!"

"Ya turkey!"

James just smiled, ducked the sneakers and flying towels, and slipped out the door.

But his smile faded as he walked on past the gym. Things were getting serious with Lacey, and sooner or later there might come the Moment of Truth. And James wasn't entirely sure he knew everything he should in order to be cool when that moment came.

"Hey, Flash!" It was Rip Lindeman, in full football regalia, jogging down the hall. "Where're those shots you promised me?"

"I've been printing them up," said James.

"How 'bout coming by tonight and bringing 'em to me?" said Rip. "Me and some of the guys are going to be at my house shooting pool and having some brews."

"Sounds great," said James.

"Okay, kid. See you tonight. Got to get to practice," and he gave James a friendly slap on the rear as he jogged out the door to the field.

James figured if anyone knew how to be cool, it would be Rip.

16.

Three older guys were shooting pool with Rip down in the finished basement of the Lindeman house.

"Hey, James," said Rip when he came down the stairs, "grab a brewski. I'll be with you soon as I finish off this bunch of amateurs."

James took off his jacket and laid the envelope with Rip's pictures on the bar. It was an actual bar, with two lamp posts on top that lit up and said "Drinks." Flashing beer signs hung on the wall behind: an electric waterfall, a revolving biplane, a cowboy. James took a can of beer from the refrigerator, which was built into the wall, and popped the top.

Rip came over, holding his cue

"Here," he said, "dig this. My father's," and plunked a glass down on the bar for James.

It was a "party glass" with a painting of a naked woman on the outside and the words "Drink Me."

James noticed that all the guys were drinking beer from these glasses. They each had a different girl with a different saying.

One of them raised his glass to James.

"Rip's Dad is a real cool guy."

James grinned and poured his beer into the glass, watching it rise around the woman. He used to have glasses with pictures painted on the outside, but they were of Bugs Bunny and Mr. Magoo.

Rip stepped up to the table and neatly sank the two-ball in the side pocket.

"Hey, you making it with that blondie cheer-leader?" one of the guys asked Rip.

"Not my style," said Rip, circling the table.

"How come?"

"Too nutty. She thinks being careful takes away the romance."

"Oh, brother," said the first guy. "Wants to play Russian Roulette, huh?"

Rip bent over the table and took aim.

"Right. And that's one game the old Ripper here doesn't play."

"Happened to a buddy of mine," one of them said. "Had to get married."

They all shook their heads.

"Ain't worth it," another guy said, as Rip ended the game with a combination shot. James stood near the bar, drinking his beer, absorbing the wisdom.

Rip handed his cue to one of the guys and came over to James. He was wearing jeans and a plaid flannel shirt tucked in, with a belt buckle as big as a fist in the shape of a lion's head.

"That's my sign," said Rip, pointing to the buckle. "I'm a Leo."

James didn't know what to say, so he handed Rip the envelope. Rip started going through the glossies. "Great shots," he said. "You got a real eye for action."

He pulled out a picture of Lacey.

"Hey, and not just in sports!"

James blushed. "Dunno how that got mixed up with yours."

"No sweat," said Rip, shuffling the photos back into a pile. "I'm starved. How about a sandwich?"

He reached into the refrigerator and pulled out a plate of sandwiches, each one neatly wrapped in waxed paper, left for him and his friends by his mother.

"I'll just have a beer," said James.

"One beer," said Rip, and he set it on the bar.

They took their beers and sat down on an old vinyl couch with stiff green cushions in the corner of the room.

Rip unwrapped his sandwich.

"Uh, Rip . . ."

"Yeah?"

"Well, I was wondering—" James took a big swig of beer. "I mean—if there's anything special you do. To score."

Rip chomped on the sandwich looked out across the room as he recited, "Don't let up. Keep 'em playing de-fense. Mix it up. Pass and then plunge."

"I meant with girls," said James.

Rip looked surprised and wiped his mouth with the back of his hand.

"Whattya think I just told ya?"

James flashed him the wide fake grin.

"Oh, yeah," he said. "Right. De-fense. Pass and then plunge."

"And always protect your flanks. I mean, no matter what *they* say, *you* be careful. Otherwise you get mousetrapped."

"Trapped," repeated James.

"You know it. Better safe than sorry."

James nodded. "Sure thing. Got it," and chugged the rest of the beer, closing his eyes so he wouldn't have to face the lady on the glass.

17.

James's father seemed to have the same message for him.

"Lacey sure is a cute girl, James," he remarked one evening after he had come up to the darkroom and peered at all the pictures of Lacey that were tacked to the wall.

"Yes, sir."

"And you can knock off that 'sir' stuff with me," his father said. "I mean, I'm a person and you're a person and I just happen to be the person who is your father, while you turn out to be the person who's my son."

James was drying some prints. He wondered what his father was getting to.

"Looks like that's how it is," said James.

"Sure," his father shrugged. "I mean, you're not a little kid anymore. That's why your mother wanted me to come and talk to you."

James pulled a print off the dryer.

"About what?" he asked.

"Well, about . . ." James's father sat down on the

folding chair. "About the fact that someday you'll be a father and you'll have kids yourself."

"Yeah?"

"Not right away, of course, you wouldn't want to get into that scene right away—But hell, I'm sure you know all about what I'm talking about."

"Oh, sure," James said, turning to look at his father. "You bet."

His father seemed relieved. He stood up and gave James a hearty slap on the back.

"Well, just remember, son, be good. And if you can't be good—be careful."

James nodded.

"Yes, sir."

"Hiya, James. We gonna play ball?"

It was Saturday and James was loading groceries into Herman's truck.

"Gotta do this first," said James.

Richie leaned his bike up against a tree.

"I'll give you a hand," he said, lifting a carton.

"You're a real pal, Richie."

James had been preoccupied all week. There was one thing on his mind: how to be careful. How to be prepared. How not to get mousetrapped. And now he had come up with a plan.

"Guess it'll be pretty tough when you move to Boston and don't have any friends," Richie said.

"Well, I'll get some, I guess."

"It'll probably take a long time," Richie said. "But at least while you're lonely and miserable, you'll know you still got good friends back here like me."

"Thanks, Richie," said James.

"You can count on it."

"I am."

"What do you mean?" Richie asked.

James stopped loading the cartons.

"Well, you've got something I need, and I know you'll let me have it 'cause you're a real true friend. Remember when we were blood brothers when we were seven?"

"Yeah, I remember," Richie said. "What thing?"

"The thing you carry around in your wallet all the time."

"My membership card in the Y?"

"No, dummy," said James, "The thing you carry around 'just in case.'"

Richie smiled slowly and patted the wallet in his hip pocket.

"You mean old 'Be Prepared'? Hey, I mean, that's valuable."

"Okay." James suddenly became businesslike. "So how much you want for it?"

Richie stepped back, his hand protecting his back pocket.

"You crazy? I got to have that with me at all times. You can't tell when something might happen."

"Has it?" asked James.

"What?"

"Happened."

Richie cocked his head, looked down the street, and frowned.

"Just because it hasn't happened as of yet," he explained, "doesn't mean it might not happen any time. I could be walkin' down Main later and some beautiful blonde stranger might give me the old look, and where would I be?"

Richie blinked.

"You take five bucks for it?"

"You can't put a price on a thing like that."

"Okay." James was determined. "My official Bobby Orr hockey stick?"

He could see Richie backing down.

"I dunno. . . ."

"*With* my regulation NHL hockey puck. A deal?"

Richie's foot scuffed the sidewalk. He considered. "I guess," he agreed at last.

James grinned and picked up a carton.

"How come you want this so bad?" Richie asked. "You and Lacey?"

"Nah," said James, shaking the hair from his eyes as he set the carton in the truck. "Just protection. I might be walking down Main later today and some beautiful blonde might—"

Richie tackled him and knocked him to the ground. They wrestled off the curb.

"Hey, boys," called Herman, coming out of the store, "no roughhouse!"

18.

The woman in the photograph wore her hair in a bun and the man was balding. They looked like they were practicing karate. The photos were muddy gray. The man and woman were poised beside each other, scarcely touching. They looked like they were wearing flesh-colored tights.

One Hundred and One Positions for Gratification.

James huddled in the back of the bookstore hoping nobody would see him flipping through the book. The captions said "Number One," "Number Two," "Number Three." All the way up to Number One Hundred and One.

Is this what it's like? He pictured himself and Lacey standing on a mat in the gym. They wore red satin wrestling shorts and white undershirts. The bell went off. Number One. They went to the mat in a head-lock. Number Two. A left arm pin. Number Three. A shoulder flip. All the way up to Number One Hundred and One, when they would rise, bow to the audience and each other, and fall back exhausted onto the cold gray mat.

"Find what you want, James?" the bookstore owner called from behind the counter.

Startled, James snapped the book shut.

19.

James and Lacey stuck to old Number One position, which was sitting together on the couch in her parents' living room.

After ten minutes of breathless kissing, Lacey pulled away.

"Sore lips," she smiled.

"Hey," said James, "it's a whole new way to baby-sit."

"Beats the back seat of cars, anyway," Lacey said. "But we have to be quiet. Don't want to wake dear sweet little brother Henry."

"That's okay," said James, pulling her toward him again. "I'd rather whisper than freeze."

"And we have at least two more hours until my folks come home," she told him, her mouth close to his.

"How come Henry's ten years younger than you?" whispered James.

Lacey shrugged. "Ask my mother." She put her arms around his neck.

"Well, you don't have to worry," said James. "A man protects the woman he loves. None of this crazy Russian Roulette stuff."

She kissed him, little kisses, all around his mouth. "My darling," she said, "my genuine love."

They kissed again, slowly, tenderly. . . .

And then they heard a high-pitched shriek right next to their ears.

They opened their eyes to see a fanged Dracula face.

It was dear sweet brother Henry, wearing his Halloween costume.

"Take that thing off, Henry," Lacey said, her arms still around James.

"You're s'posed to be sittin' with me, not sittin' with him," Henry whined through the mask.

"You're s'posed to be in bed, asleep, ya little nerd," said James.

Henry began to cry. "I'm gonna tell! I'm gonna tell on you to Mom and Dad!"

"Okay, Henry, okay," Lacey untangled herself and got up. "We'll all watch TV. Together." With a forlorn look at her lover, James, she went to turn it on.

"What was the key to the Allied victory?" Miss Moger was asking. Behind her a large map of Europe was studded with arrows and pins.

The class did not respond. Half sat with their heads resting in their hands. In the back row, some boys were trading Vampirella comics and James was trying to do his Spanish homework.

"The key was the Blitz," Richie answered.

"The Blitz was the Nazis, Richard," Miss Moger said. "They were on the other side."

She looked around at the class and leaned forward on her desk with both hands.

"The key to the joint Allied victory, class, was *planning!* Without successful *planning,* all the guns and bombs would have gone for naught."

James looked up from his Spanish homework. Lacey turned back to him at the same instant and smiled.

"Now, class, what was the key to victory?"

James and Lacey kept looking at each other and smiling as they chanted along with the rest of the class. *"Planning!"*

20.

"So what *is* the plan?" Lacey asked, as they walked hand-in-hand down the steps of the school that afternoon.

"The campsite."

"How do we get there?"

"Last time we went out, we drove up the Interstate, but you and me can take our bikes and go up old Route 6. It's about five miles and then a half-mile on the dirt road, then there's a pile of stones that marks the back trail up Mount Kasamoka."

"You sure you know how to get there?"

"Trust me," said James.

"You know I trust you," Lacey said, slipping her arm in his. They turned the corner, away from the crowd. "But don't you think it'll be cold?"

"Sure. But that's even better. That means there won't be anyone else up there for miles. We'll be totally alone. Just dress warm."

He stopped and turned to her.

"It's okay," he assured her. "We love each other."

"We love each other," Lacey nodded. "And if we have to freeze, then we'll freeze. They just didn't give us any time."

"I know," said James. "We'll do whatever we have to do. Nothing can stop us now."

They embraced. Over her shoulder, above the tops of the houses and the white church steeple, he could see the shape of Mount Kasamoka in the foothills of the Cascade Range looming in the distance.

21.

They looked like they were going to Alaska.

They wore down-filled parkas, woolen scarves over their faces, knit hats, gloves, heavy jeans, and hiking boots with two pair of socks. They carried orange nylon knapsacks on their backs filled with bottles of water, a road map, Granola bars, pocket knives, matches, and an orange. Each had one half of a double-size sleeping bag strapped to the back of the bike in a roll.

They headed east out of town, a mile or so along the Interstate, then turned off on a two-lane road. It seemed a lot wider and a lot longer on bicycles. Cars passed quickly and they had to ride single-file.

The sun had been out when they left but now it was sealed in by fog. The sky was uniformly gray and they could smell dampness in the air. It brought up the scent of dead leaves and drying streams from the woods near the road; when they passed through farmland the wind came strong and cold over the barren fields.

"How're you doing?" James called.

"Okay," Lacey said, half-turning back to him. "It's getting hot in this jacket."

"Take it off."

"Then I'll freeze."

"The radio said it might snow tonight," said James, squinting at the bright blank sky. "At least frost."

"I can see it now," she called back to him breathlessly. " 'Young Couple Buried in Snowstorm'!"

After two hours of hard pedaling they came to the dirt road. It was difficult to ride the ten-speeds over the rocks and clumps of frozen ground, so they ended up walking the bikes the last half-mile.

No cars passed on this road. The woods on either side of them were almost colorless. Without leaves the trees made a delicate network of bare branches like a haze receding into the darkness of the mountainside. The signs for trails had all been taken down for the winter and the gates to a parking area were chained shut. It was quiet and the cold air was still.

At the sign of three large rocks piled on top of each other, Lacey and James locked their bicycles to a young tree. They began to climb the trail toward the campsite where the Hunter family had had its last cookout. Their breath hung in the air before them. The season's layer of dead branches and leaves crackled beneath their feet.

"This is it," James announced when they had reached the campsite.

"It's nice," Lacey said, looking down at the ravine and feeling a cold draft of wind rushing through it. Above them trees swayed suddenly.

James was kicking loose stones away from the flat area near the blackened fire site and unfurling his sleeping bag on the ground. Lacey did the same and they zipped them together.

They looked at each other over the tops of their scarves. Only their eyes showed beneath the knit wool caps. Their noses were red.

"Prepare for entry," said James.

They knelt beside each other, awkward in the heavy clothing, and began to peel off layers. They had turned their backs to each other, discarding jackets, hats, scarves, sweaters, boots . . . When Lacey had stripped down to a T-shirt and jeans, she was shaking so badly from the cold that she had to slip inside the sleeping bag.

"It's freezing in here!" she exclaimed. Her teeth were chattering.

"It'll warm up," James assured her. He was still wearing his flannel shirt and jeans as he stuck his legs into the bag.

"C'mere, quick!" Lacey squealed, reaching for him.

"You sound like a woodpecker," James said, holding her tight.

"I—I c—can't help i—it," Lacey stammered; her whole body was trembling with cold.

"We should have built a fire," said James. Inside the bag their bare feet touched, freezing.

"That would have helped."

"It'll warm up," said James again.

"Promise?"

"Promise."

And he began to kiss her quivering lips.

"Oh, my God!" he cried suddenly, breaking away to roll on his back and stare up at the bare trees.

"What's w—wrong?"

"I forgot something," he said. "The most important part. In my knapsack."

"You'll freeze if you go out there," Lacey said.

James tightened his lips, then threw the bag open.

"I shall return!" He crawled out and hopped across the campsite on bare feet to his knapsack. Lacey was now completely inside the sleeping bag. James could see just a few strands of blonde hair.

He rummaged through the bag, found Richie's little packet of protection in the inside zipper pocket, and danced back to the sleeping bag. He brushed twigs from his feet and thrust them inside.

"You *did* freeze!" Lacey said from deep inside the bag.

"I'll thaw," said James, inching toward her. But now he was trembling too.

She poked her head out of the top.

"I'll try to help," she said, and grabbed him around the neck like a life raft in icy seas.

22.

By the time they were dressed and packed and walking down the trail, the temperature had dropped five degrees.

"The only flaw in the plan was the weather," said James. "It beat Napoleon and Hitler, too, on the Russian front."

"Too cold," Lacey said, shaking her head and watching the trail.

"I don't know," said James. "It looks so easy in the movies."

"Sure, when you have a terrific bedroom with silk sheets, or a terrific field of daisies in summer. They never do it on the freezingest day of the year, in a sleeping bag, when it's both of their first times."

James sniffed. "Cold weather can whip anyone. That's why the Allies had D-Day in June."

"They didn't take chances."

"All we have to do is have our same plan but when it gets warm out. Then it would work."

He held back the whippy branches of rhododendron as she ducked past.

"But you'll be gone by then," Lacey reminded him.

"I'll come back. I'll come back to see you in spring and get a job for the summer."

"Really?" she said. "You will?"

They climbed over a fallen log.

"Will you really wait?" said James. "Wait for me. Until it's warm."

"Of course I'll wait."

"I'll come back the first warm day," James said.

"The first warm day here, or the first warm day in Boston?"

"Whichever comes first."

The ground had leveled out and they could walk side by side.

"How will you know?" Lacey asked.

"I'll watch *The Today Show*. When they have the national weather map."

"I'll watch too. Every day. So I'll know when you're coming."

Lacey stopped walking and turned to James.

She picked a leaf from the fold of his wool hat.

"I love you," she said. "And I want it to be you. To be the first one."

"Oh Lace," he cried, his heart soaring, "I love you too."

Soon they would unlock their bicycles for the long ride to town in the gathering dark. But for that moment they could stand at the edge of the woods on the deserted road and kiss for a long time and nothing mattered except the feel and taste and warmth of each other's lips. They could smell the approach of winter and feel it in their frozen fingertips and toes. Their parkas were bulky; Lacey's hat slipped off as James put his hands in her hair. Behind them the last dull yellow leaves of a maple tree fluttered slowly to the ground.

23.

The realtor had driven a stake into the center of the Hunter family's front lawn. "Sold."

James gave it a kick as he crossed the lawn for the fortieth time that morning. James was pacing as his parents went back and forth between the front door and the car, loading up the last of their possessions.

His whole life had gone into four big cardboard cartons which had been shipped the day before. He had to give up some of his favorite childhood things like his science kit, his rock collection, and an assortment of model cars; all the old toys had been given to Goodwill. What was left was packed into four boxes labeled "James" and loaded into the van along with cartons marked "Dishes," "Books," and "Living room."

Richie came walking down the street on his way to school. They had decided that when they graduated high school they would go to the same college, so they figured they only had two years to go. Richie told

James that when he came back for his job in the summer he could live with Richie and his parents.

"You'll probably be a snob, living in Boston," Richie said, standing in front of James, holding his books.

"Well at least I won't be a hick."

"Snob."

"Hick."

They began to punch each other, back and forth, in the arm, until James suddenly changed tactics and jumped on Richie, pinning him to the ground.

"Hey. I'll be late for class."

"This time I give you your freedom, Redskin," James said, letting him up.

"Next time I have your scalp, Paleface," Richie said. He stood there for a moment, awkwardly, looking at James and then at the ground. And then he said, "See ya around," and turned to walk away, looking back only once to give James the "Beaver Face" before running off to school.

James spun around and gave the realtor's sign another kick, knocking it over on its side. He walked toward the house and met his father who was coming out, carrying a suitcase in each hand.

"Not much time, James," he said.

"I know."

At the doorstep, James realized he had nothing to go back into the house for and he turned around and paced back toward the sidewalk. Lacey was crossing the street, her hands deep in her pockets, her hat pulled down over her eyes. She wore a wool shirt and red down-filled vest.

"Hi."

"You're not going to school?" said James.

"I couldn't."

"Come inside a second," he said.

His father was making another trip, this time with a shopping bag crammed with coat hangers.

"Hi, Lacey," he said. "Five more minutes, James."

They walked into the empty living room. It was echoey and strange. There were dark spots on the walls where pictures and mirrors had been hanging for over fifteen years.

"It looks so cold and empty." Lacey shivered.

"Maybe I could hide out somewhere," said James. "At the next gas station I could jump out and run away to a deserted farmhouse. You could meet me there."

"We'd get arrested," Lacey said.

"I guess so. You can't beat Them."

They stood in silence.

Lacey sat down on the floor, cross-legged, head in hand.

"Stay like that," said James, going for his camera bag near the door. "I want to take your picture there."

But when he looked through the camera he saw her sitting on the old living room couch; the room was filled with furniture, as cozy as always. Lacey, in a long Edwardian robe, was darning a pair of his socks and behind her a fire blazed.

"Too bad your family had to move," she said in the dream, "but it was sweet of them to give us the house to live in."

"I told them in no uncertain terms," said James, who saw himself sitting at her feet on a bearskin rug, "that these were the only conditions under which I'd finish my education. They had no choice."

"Let's call for some hot buttered rum," Lacey said, "and then to bed. . . ."

James snapped the picture, the real one, of Lacey sitting forlornly on the bare floor in her stocking cap and jeans as his mother stuck her head in the front door and called, "Let's go, James. We're leaving now."

James held out his hands and pulled Lacey up.

"I can't stand it," she said, bursting into tears. He put his arm around her as they walked to the door.

The family car was parked at the end of the walk, all packed, motor running, ready to go.

James and Lacey stood for a moment on the doorstep in the gray daylight. She looked at him with bright wet eyes.

"I'll just go home and start waiting for you," she said, raising a crumpled tissue to her nose. Then she turned and ran across the lawn to the sidewalk and down the street.

"I love you, Lacey!" James called after her, "I love you now and always! For keeps!"

Cramped in the back seat with boxes, suitcases, plants, bags, and his sister, James stared out like a prisoner being hauled away to jail.

"There goes the library," Sandy said. "Goodbye. There goes the Galaxy Diner. Goodbye. There goes Herman's Super-ette. Goodbye."

"For Heaven's sake." Their father sounded exasperated. "We're off on a new adventure. Think of that. Think of what's ahead. Don't look back."

Sandy and James watched as the town they had grown up in quickly slipped away. At last they were at the edge of it, past the train station and the old sawmill, and the sign that said "WELCOME, DRIVE CAREFULLY."

"There goes the town," Sandy said, "goodbye," and

she twisted in her seat to lean over between her parents and watch out the front windshield.

But James remained staring fiercely out the back window. He had another mission now.

"*I shall return!*" he said.

PART TWO

24.

At a Howard Johnson's on the Massachusetts Turnpike their mother ordered a New England clam roll.

"Might as well go with the natives," she said.

The clam roll turned out to be a hot-dog bun stuffed with rubbery strings supposed to be New England fried clams, and James and Sandy were glad they had ordered regular Oregon-type cheeseburgers.

The "Mass Pike," a fast no-nonsense road bisecting the state, took them straight from the Berkshires to Boston. There wasn't much to look at along the way: empty forests, spinning gas station signs indicating towns off the exits, dirty shrunken piles of snow along the sides of the road.

The approach to the city was clogged with traffic and it seemed every hundred feet there was another billboard advertising a hotel or a brand of cigarettes. They passed through a toll booth and found themselves riding along the Charles River with the city on their right.

"It's pretty," said their mother.

The sun sparkled off the water and the low red-brick town houses of Back Bay looked old and quaint. People were jogging and riding bicycles along the path by the river where the snow had melted. Across the water on the Cambridge side they could see the domes of M.I.T.

The Hunters had time to enjoy the beauty of this clear winter day because they were stuck in a massive traffic jam on Storrow Drive.

"We're trapped," James moaned, slumping down in the back seat.

"We just happened to arrive at rush hour," said his father.

"If we get a flat tire we'll be doomed for sure," Sandy said.

The traffic began to move and they found themselves going up a ramp leading over a bridge and water.

"I didn't say to go left," said their mother, trying to find their position on a road map, "I just asked if we should."

"Too late now," said their father. "When you said left, I went left."

"I think we just missed the city," said James, when they passed a sign indicating "New Hampshire, Points North."

They got off the bridge, circled around along a truck route, and came back. This time as they crossed the bridge they had a spectacular view of downtown Boston: church towers with golden clocks set against glass sky-scrapers, old colonial buildings of red brick contrasting with the sweeping modern architecture of the new Government Center. The sun set the city in sharp relief, and as they headed along an elevated highway, their mother repeated, "It *really* is pretty."

They turned off at a sign that promised "Downtown," but found themselves on a bumpy road following the waterfront, where sailboats were docked in private marinas and huge tankers and tugboats maneuvered in the choppy blue harbor beyond. They drove slowly past renovated warehouses which had been converted into expensive-looking apartments, restaurants, and shops. In front of a fish market with signs that advertised fresh lobster and cod, a wheelbarrow filled with ice sparkled like diamonds in the sun. Sea gulls screeched above them and the air smelled of old wood and salt.

"Well," said their father, "here we are at Boston Harbor."

"Why?" asked his wife. They had been driving in desperate circles around Boston for an hour and a half, all the time within a two-mile radius of their goal.

"You're beginning to sound like Sandy," he replied.

"I mean, why are we at the harbor?" she asked.

"We're getting our bearings," he said, making a sudden left turn down a quay with an old shipping building and nautical shops. The road ended abruptly at a barrier. They were facing the water and could go no further. The city was behind them.

"We're lost," James pronounced.

After a conference, a bathroom stop at a gas station, some Cokes, and the determination to "bear down," "get organized," "get this thing over with," and "not make any more dumb mistakes," the Hunter family, with the help of two separate police cruisers and a friendly passer-by with an Afghan hound, negotiated an intricate path from Boston's waterfront to the Back Bay.

Until a hundred years ago the Back Bay was swampland. It had been filled in and carefully designed to be an ornamental section of the city, incorporating public buildings, churches, and mansions. Rows of town houses were built in styles from Greek Revival to Academic Brick. They were generally three stories high, narrow, with bowed windows and steps leading to recessed doorways with wrought iron-and-glass doors. First built for well-to-do families, they now housed a mixture of young professionals living in apartments and condominiums, transients in rooming houses, and college students.

Marlborough Street was well-maintained. Rows of bay windows overlooked the quiet street which was lined with trees and authentic-looking gas lamps. To an urbanite moving from a larger city, Marlborough Street would seem an oasis of quaint architecture and homes scaled to a smaller, Victorian view of human life—a respite from high-rise apartment living.

To James and Sandy, moving from a sprawling house on a half-acre of land, it looked like a concrete jungle.

They double-parked in front of their new home. It was a neat but worn three-story, with a scrawny tree in a tiny space of dirt bounded by a curb that was the front yard. The steps leading to the heavy wrought iron door were chipped and in need of paint. The twin downstairs windows were filmed with soot. A torn yellow shade hung halfway down, like the droop of one palsied eyelid.

"That's no house," said James.

"It's a grungy old apartment building," Sandy complained.

"It happens to be called a *town house*," said her mother. "Your father explained it to you in great detail."

She pushed down on the door-handle to get out.

Dad was already up the steps, fiddling with the key.

Their mother stepped out of the car and held the seat forward, but the two remained in back, sulking.

"Now come on, let's go in and look and give it a chance. With an *open mind*. Got that, gang?"

Sandy and James climbed out reluctantly.

"My mind's a blank," said James.

25.

They didn't have heat, electricity, or hot water their first night on Marlborough Street. They huddled in front of the fireplace in winter jackets, sitting on foam-rubber camping mattresses. The house felt big and strange around them, with two silent floors of darkness above. They unwrapped sandwiches they had purchased at a greasy shop around the corner, as their father pushed some odd scraps of paper against a half-burned log left in the fireplace to make a fire.

"I hereby christen our new home with its first fire," he said. "May we have many more, and much warmth and brightness in our new life here." He struck a match and started a small creeping flame.

"Hurrah and second the motion," cheered their mother, raising a drippy sandwich in salute.

"May we also have heat, hot water, and electricity," Sandy added.

"We'll have them by this time tomorrow," said her father, leaning forward to blow on the small flame, "so try to be brave." Charred bits of paper flew up the chimney.

"When our furniture gets here, you'll all feel at home," his wife added.

Their father stood up. "Got to find something more to burn," he said, and took his flashlight to explore the upper floors.

"How about burning the house?" muttered James, who was certain he had never felt so lonely and displaced in his life.

"Please," said his mother, "give it a chance."

His father returned in a few moments with an orange crate covered with spider webs.

"Found it in a closet," he said, breaking it apart. Soon they had a real fire.

James leaned his head on his knapsack and lay down with his boots near the fireplace. "Why couldn't we have gotten the same kind of house we had back home instead of this weird kind?" he said, staring into the flames.

"It's not weird," said his father. "It's different. That's what's nice about it."

"What's so nice about different?" asked James. "Freaks are different."

"James," said his father, "you're becoming a reactionary. An old stick-in-the mud before your time."

"He is," said Sandy. "He's boring. He only orders vanilla."

"Better than that ripple-crunch-goo-stuff you get and never finish," James argued, rising up on an elbow, "and get all over yourself like a *tomboy*."

"Finish your submarine sandwich," interrupted his father.

"It isn't a 'submarine,'" said James. "It's a 'hero.'"

"In Boston they call it a submarine. Or a sub."

"Well, they're calling it wrong."

"Maybe they'll think *you're* wrong, James," said his mother. "Ever think of that?"

"Couldn't care less."

"You'd care if you met some girl like Lacey here and you wanted to impress her and make her think about you the way Lacey used to," Sandy said.

James stood up. He threw his sandwich into the fire.

"Lacey *still* thinks about me the same way and *I* still think about her the same way and we always will and I couldn't care less about some stupid Boston girl who thinks 'heros' are 'submarines,'" he said, and stalked out of the room.

Upstairs it was musty and cold. Using a camping flashlight, James found a door halfway ajar and pushed it open. This would be his room for the night.

He imagined as he opened the door he found not emptiness, but an exotic room filled with palm trees and rich fabrics draping the walls like a tent, lit by candles in tall holders that stood on the floor, with incense burning and the sound of a lute. Lacey Stevens smiled at him from a gold divan where she reclined like Cleopatra, in an Egyptian robe of gold and black, her feet in tiny sandals, arms wound with gold serpent bracelets, eyes black and shining in the candlelight. She would reach out for him, fingers in jeweled rings, all languorous and perfumed, as, dumbfounded, he approached her side.

"What—why—how did you get here?" James asked.

"I am here because you are here, my darling," Queen Lacey replied. Her fingertips were insistent on his wrists, pulling him slowly toward her and down.

"But how did you get away from school—your par-

ents—how did you get here from Oregon?" he asked,
sinking to his knees on the leopard rug.

"Love conquers all, my darling," she whispered into
his burning ear.

The long wail of a fire engine brought James slowly
out of his fantasy like a sleeper returning to conscious-
ness from the sweet depths of a dream. He didn't
want to awaken. He didn't want to find himself in a
barren room, alone, three thousand miles from home.

26.

"Where's the rest of the campus?" James asked his father. "The trees and football fields and dorms and stuff."

They were standing on a corner in Back Bay a few streets from their house. A wooden sign stuck in a garden said "Hastings College." And screwed into the brick of a building, a brass plaque: "Department of Humanities."

"This is a *city* college," his father said.

"You mean it's not a *real* college."

"Of course it's real," said his father. He was holding the new leather briefcase his wife had given him as a congratulations gift. The briefcase didn't match his overcoat and creased corduroys; their clothes and furniture had still not arrived from Oregon.

"Say, Hunter," said a tall man with white hair and a ruddy face, "didn't expect you heah till tomorrow. Welcome to Hastings."

He spoke in a strange flat-sounding accent.

"Thanks. Got here yesterday. This is my son, James. This is Professor Flaherty. Ancient History, right?"

The professor held out a beefy hand for James to shake. He wore an orange arctic jacket trimmed with fur and carried a battered old briefcase.

"The oldah the bettah," he said. "How are you finding our faih city, son?"

"Looks pretty old to me," said James.

"You'll have to come out and visit us in the suburbs," Flaherty said. "We're in Winchestah."

"Sounds terrific," said James's father. "Do us good to get out. Just name the day. Or night."

There was a pause. James zipped his jacket higher against the chill.

"Whenever you say . . ." his father went on awkwardly, hopefully.

Flaherty smiled. "Ah, well, soon as you get settled," he said, with a wave to a student passing by. "Maybe when it gets wahm, we can put on a bahbacue outdoors. No rush."

He began to move off.

"Oh, no," said James's father. "No rush. Of course not."

James was beginning to feel embarrassed for his father.

"It's a date, then," said Flaherty. "Lookin' fohward to it," and he hurried down the street.

James and his father walked slowly in the opposite direction.

"One of the best Ancient civ men in the country," his father remarked.

"Is that how come he talks funny?" asked James.

"He just has a Boston accent. You'll get used to it."

James looked up at his father as they walked. Crowds of students were coming out the doors. ·

"You got any friends here, Dad?" he asked.

"What do you mean? You just met one. Flaherty."

"He's not a friend like your friends back home."

"It takes time, James, for all of us."

They walked in silence. As they stopped at a corner and waited for a traffic light to change, James said, "Hey, Dad. I'm sorry. You know?"

"For what?"

"I mean, I guess you've got problems too. Changing your whole life around."

"Well, we're all in this together," his father replied. He seemed to grip his briefcase tighter.

The city wind blew James's hair. He could feel pieces of dirt in it and he lowered his eyes.

"Well, I'm sorry, Dad," he repeated, "I'll try not to be such a nerd."

He felt his father's hand on his shoulder as they crossed the street.

"Just do your best," he said.

27.

The steel doors of James's new school had been patched over many times with metal sheets; they were warped and battered as if people had been kicking and blasting and firing guns at the school. Spray-can graffiti covered the lower walls in the yard and an American flag, in tatters, flew from a second story. The windows all were barred.

His mother had driven him there and dropped him off at the high iron gate. James climbed the steps alone, carrying a new spiral notebook. A mix of voices—classes in unison, teachers droning, a high-pitched laugh—seemed to seep through the old walls.

James pulled hard on the heavy doors and entered a vestibule.

There he imagined a welcome committee of bugles and drums as the high school band stood in the hallway before him and cheerleaders did cartwheels, yelling,

"Who's a man?
Who's a man?

James! James! James!"

He saw himself smiling and waving to a crowd of well-dressed kids who cheered until he silenced them by stepping up to a microphone and making a short speech.

"I want to thank you all, and pledge that I will perform here to my fullest abilities as athlete, scholar, and friend to all people!"

The crowd cheered again and picked him up on their shoulders to carry him in triumph down the hall, past friendly teachers waving to him from the doorways of their classrooms, past girls who jumped up and down and swooned . . .

The bell rang, a shattering alarm that made James jump back to the reality of the dingy green hallway with brown tiled floors, lit by yellow globe lamps that somehow made everything seem darker.

Doors opened and classes came pouring into the halls. He noticed with uneasiness that all the boys were wearing coats and ties.

James tried to walk casually down the hall but he was conspicuous in his winter jacket and single notebook. He was stared at and giggled at and received intentional bumps on the arm as boys rushed past.

"Hey, look what we got here, Dick," said one to his friend, "a real derry!"

The two stopped James in an alcove near the stairway.

"Nah, he's just new," said the other. "Right, kid?"

"Yeah," said James. "I just got here. From Oregon."

"Orry-gon?" said the first. "They got derries out there?"

Tom had long brown hair and wore a black sports coat and narrow tie which seemed to have been passed down from an older brother who had gone to the same school in another era.

"What's a derry?" asked James.

"Derry, like in derelict," said Tom. "A slob. A bum. A guy that's baked all the time."

"Baked?"

"Don't they have weed out there?" asked Dick, whose stringy reddish hair reached his shoulders. He wore a wide tie and plaid jacket, as if in imitation of a father or uncle, a salesman maybe, who liked his beer. Dick himself had a bit of a belly.

"You know," he said. "Weed to smoke and get baked on."

"Oh," said James with a smile, "you mean *fried*."

"Fried!" Tom exclaimed nudging his friend with an elbow. "How 'bout that? Must be the hick name for baked."

James's smile faded.

"Never mind him," said Dick, hooking his hair behind an ear. "You wanna start out here right?"

James nodded.

"Then split for today and show up tomorrow in a nice tie and jacket, okay? You'll be one of the crowd. Like everyone else."

"Yeah," said James, relieved, "thanks a lot."

"Don't mention it," said Dick, as James pushed through the swinging doors, down the steps to the street. He didn't look back to see Tom and Dick break up laughing the moment he left.

He began to walk. Soon he was out of the neighborhood of the school, heading toward the heart of the city. He made no effort to get his bearings; the streets seemed to be in no order at all, so he let himself wander, turning corners when he felt like it, attracted by something in a store window or simply pushed by the crowds.

It was lunchtime and the streets were busy. Everyone who hurried past him seemed to have a purpose; he had none. It felt strange to be out of school in the middle of the day.

He found himself in a three-block section of dirty bookstores, adult movies with enticing titles, and nightclubs that advertised with lavender silhouettes of naked women. He stopped to stare at a photograph of a woman with tassels hanging from her breasts.

"Never again," said a voice, close.

James looked up.

"Never again, I tell ya."

He was confronted by a crazy man with bulgy suspicious eyes, wearing a lopsided hat and filthy jacket.

The man grabbed James by the shoulder.

"Tell 'em not to do it, son," he croaked.

James saw the stubble and sores on the man's face and a cut on his forehead crusted over with blood. He broke away and ran. The man remained in the middle of the sidewalk, talking and gesturing to himself.

That's a derry, thought James, walking quickly through crowds of people who he now noticed *all* had suspicious eyes; they were carrying battered shopping bags, wearing rags, raving by themselves in doorways beneath neon signs which promised "All-Nude College Girl Revue." They called this section the Combat Zone, and James was relieved to be heading out of it.

A slant of sunlight poured between two department stores illuminating throngs of people passing between Winter and Washington Streets, the most congested corner in the city. He felt like he was in the bottom of a canyon, looking up at facades of buildings forty years old, with outmoded signs of stores long gone, covered over with bright graphic announcements of the new. The layering and changing of businesses over the years showed clearly in the strata of signs on this street. At the intersection, a mounted police-woman directed pedestrians and cars, the horse stamping and turning in tight circles in the center of the crowd.

James bought a hot dog from a man with a cart and continued past jewelry stores, jeans stores, shops that sold small appliances at discount prices, shoe stores, a joke shop, until he found more evidence of the city's evolution: an old graveyard with paths and trees, set between two office buildings. A painted sign at the gate said "Granery Burying Grounds" and listed Paul Revere and Ben Franklin's parents as occupants.

He turned in, walking past thin worn headstones which were leaning at odd angles. They carried faded inscriptions left two hundred and three hundred years before of colonists who had died from pneumonia or in Indian attacks or in the Revolutionary War. He sat down on a little curb in a patch of sunlight. Tremont Street was only fifty yards away, jammed with traffic, but it seemed sealed off by the iron gates from the timelessness of the graveyard.

James opened his new notebook to the first page and brought a pen from his pocket.

He wrote, *"Dear Lacey . . ."*

Behind him a Parks Department man wearing a red sweater was sweeping litter down the path with short strokes of a push broom. The rhythmic sweep of the broom and the rustling of a squirrel in the leaves nearby were the only sounds James heard as he remembered how it felt to kiss Lacey at the foot of the trail on Mount Kasamoka when the air smelled wet with snow.

"*It sure is cold here,* he wrote, *and I can't wait for the first warm day so I can come out to see you like we planned. What do you consider warm? Anything over freezing? Ha ha. Your devoted lover, James.*".

He closed the notebook and slipped his hands into his pockets. He was content to be among the tombstones and bones of historic ancestors while the people of the city went by outside the gates in a brightly-changing wash. Then the sun was covered by a cloud and it became too cold to sit still.

28.

It took two days for the heat, hot water, and electricity to start working at the Hunter house. And still the moving van had not arrived.

Years of camping out had made them resourceful. James's mother improvised by cooking over the kerosene stove in the kitchen. They bought dried eggs and canned sausage and ate as if it were breakfast in the mountains of Oregon—except they were standing in the bare cold kitchen of a Boston town house, with empty white cabinets that needed dishes, a linoleum floor that needed washing, and a glaring overhead light that needed a shade.

"Have you really emphasized the dire nature of our plight to the moving company?" James's mother asked her husband.

"I called them four times yesterday," he said. "What else can I do? Call the Justice Department?"

"You better," Sandy said, "'cause I need my football stuff. This girl I sit by, Amanda, plays pulling guard. She's terrific. She chews a whole pack of gum at once."

"That sounds nice, Sandy," said her mother, pouring hot water from a saucepan to a paper cup to make instant coffee. "Did you make any friends, James?" she asked.

"We got out early," James replied.

"Well, it takes a while to get the feel of a new school," his father said.

"Everyone going to school should exit now," said his mother, replacing the pan on the Coleman stove. "It's getting late."

Sandy bent over, let her arms dangle toward the floor, and shuffled slowly from the room, making sounds like an ape.

Her father threw his paper plate into the trash.

James remained leaning against a wall. He was methodically breaking the tines of a blue plastic fork against his plate.

"James? Don't you have to take any books to school?"

He did not look up.

"I can't go," he said.

His father turned from the door in surprise.

"What?"

"I can't go to school."

"Why not?" asked his mother.

"I don't have a jacket and tie."

"What does that have to do with it?"

"You gotta wear a jacket and tie in this crummy school," said James.

"Are you sure?"

"Sure I'm sure. All the guys had 'em on except me."

"Why didn't you tell us yesterday?" said his mother.

"We could have run out to a store and bought something for you."

"I thought the moving van might come with all our stuff in it," said James, whose fork was now a blue plastic stump.

"Well, that's the way it is," said his father. "All my stuff's in it, too, except what I've got on."

"I guess you'd better take it off," Mom said.

"What?"

"So James can have a jacket and tie so he can go to school."

"It won't fit," said James.

"It's better than nothing," she said. "Better than missing one of the first days at your new school. Right, Alan?"

His father looked at him and sighed, then began to loosen his tie.

"Right," he said. "You want to get off to a good start."

"It's going to be about four miles too big," said James.

"Here," said his father, holding out the clothes. "Just stand up tall and throw your shoulders back. No one will notice."

Everybody noticed. For one thing the jacket hung well below James's knees and covered his hands like the costume of a silent movie clown. And for another, not one of the boys in school that day was wearing a jacket and tie.

He didn't know what the trick had been, but he felt as if the whole school, 1,242 kids, had conspired to humiliate and embarrass James Hunter from Oregon.

"Hey, look!" drawled Tom, coming up to James as he huddled at his locker.

James took off his father's jacket.

"Thanks a lot, you guys," he said.

"No use trying to explain to a derry," laughed Dick. "Get a load of his disguise, will ya? Must have got it off some big old derelict passed out in a doorway."

James could feel his face grow hot.

Dick waved to some other passing students and three or four gathered around, including a black guy named Roland Banks who looked pretty fierce, with an Afro comb sticking out of his back pocket and a thin moustache over his lips.

"Hey, kid," Tom asked, "what's your thing? I mean, besides hanging around like an old derelict. You play ball, play cards, crack the books?"

The students were pressing closer around James. His back was against the cold metal door of the locker. He sensed it—there was going to be a fight.

"Maybe he's just a plain derry," said Dick. "Can't do nothing but bum around. That about it, kid?"

"You don't do nothin', huh?" said Tom.

James felt a surge of adrenaline shooting up his spine to his head. He became dizzy with it, reckless. He'd take 'em all.

"I can swim!" he shouted, fists clenched at his side.

The boys broke up laughing, slapping their knees and jabbing each other in the ribs.

"He can swim!" sputtered Dick.

"Let's throw him in the Charles, see if he sinks!"

He took it while they laughed, standing firm. His heart was racing, his body felt numb. The bell rang and the boys moved off, some of them pretending to do the breast stroke as they walked. They continued to laugh and swim all the way down the hall, their voices echoing.

James turned and walked in the opposite direction. He would not cry. He clenched his jaws.

"Hey." It was Roland strolling up beside him. "You swim for real?"

James took a breath and looked at him.

"I was on the team where I went to school before this, out in Oregon."

"So why don't you go to the pool and try out?" Roland suggested.

"Where is it?"

"In the gym, where'd you think?"

"Yeah," James felt some of his confidence returning, "I figured. But I mean, where's the gym?"

"Over in the Fenway," Roland said. "Cross town."

"How come it's not in the school?"

"No room. This here's the city, man. You go to some small town school out there in Ohio?"

"Oregon."

"Yeah. They have any bloods out there?"

"Bloods?"

"Yeah. Bloods. Brothers. Like me. Black."

"Sure," said James as they walked through a pair of swinging doors. "A'course we had 'em."

"Where'd you have 'em?" Roland asked with a little smile. "You got some little ghetto out there?"

"On TV," said James, trying to be funny. "That's where we had 'em."

"Too much!" Roland said, shaking his head. "You kept 'em locked up in the little old tube, huh?"

"No," said James, "I mean—I didn't mean—"

"Hey, it's cool, man," Roland said. "And, oh yeah, let me clue you." He pointed his finger at James. "They just run that tie and jacket number the first day of a new semester."

"I get it," said James. "Thanks."

Roland nodded and started to walk away.

"No sweat," he said.

"Hey!" James called after him, "How do I get there? Cross town. To the Fenway."

" 'Less you got wheels," Roland said, turning to walk backward a few steps, "take the 'T.' How else?"

James stood alone in the hall. "The 'T'?"

The "T" turned out to be the MBTA—Boston's public transit system—a complex of rushing crowds, screeching subway trains, confusing maps in bright colors that led to mysterious and exotic locations such as "Maverick," "Aquarium," "Riverside," and "Harvard Square." None of it made any sense to James. The only time he had had to take public transportation was when he took a bus to a dentist in the next town when his parents were too busy to drive.

It was like a nightmare. The city and its crazy trains were impossible to understand. All he wanted was to hit the water in a swimming pool to show these guys who he was and what he could do, but he spent the next two hours riding trains, getting misinformation, not understanding the conductors. It was rush hour, and most of the time he had to stand jammed up against strangers in closer physical contact than he'd ever had with anyone.

At last, in the Park Street Station he approached the person in the change booth, an older woman wearing a saggy sweater, gold wig, and blue MBTA hat.

"Can you help me, please?" he asked, putting his face, now smeared with subway grime, close to the bars of the window.

"Where do you want to go, son?" she asked.

"Oregon!" said James.

29.

It was dark by the time James returned home. He opened the front door with his new key to hear his parents' voices from the living room.

"How the hell was I supposed to know the moving van would arrive this afternoon?" his father was saying. "Couldn't you have called me at the college?"

James sat down quietly on the front hall steps.

"I did call," said his mother. "I hung on for twenty minutes and the woman said you couldn't come to the phone."

"Well, I never got the message. No one told me. Or I would have come home."

"It wouldn't have done any good anyway," said his mother. "By the time you got to the bank it would have been closed."

"Weren't they supposed to call first?"

"Yes. They were supposed to call so we could have a check ready."

"I know," interrupted his father. "Two thousand sixty dollars."

"There was a strange charge," said his mother. "Now it's two thousand four hundred dollars."

"Why didn't you write a check?"

"They wouldn't take one. They only take cash or certified money orders."

"Terrific," said his father. "I'll have to go to the bank in the morning. What time are they coming to-morrow?"

James, still listening from the steps, unzipped his jacket and rubbed a hand through his hair.

"They're not coming tomorrow. They're going to Baltimore."

"Baltimore? We don't live in Baltimore."

"The Browns do."

"Who the hell are the Browns?"

"The other people with furniture in the van."

James felt a tinge of fear at hearing his parents talk this way, with bitterness and accusation in their voices. He wondered if this was the way people fight when they're going to get a divorce.

"You have got to do something," insisted his father, "I can't live in this disarray."

"*You* can't?" His mother's voice was rising now. "What about me and the children? This house is mired in layers of nineteenth-century grime! I've been clean-ing for a week and haven't made a dent. You go off to your nice Ivy League college . . ."

"You mean ivy-*covered*," his fathered interrupted.

". . . While I'm trapped here, not knowing any-body, no friends, trying to deal with two unhappy lonely children who miss their small friendly town and their friends, confused by a big city . . ." She stopped. "*You're* the one who wanted to live in the glamorous city of Boston. You know how I felt about it. Why couldn't we live in the suburbs?"

"The suburbs?"

"What's wrong with the suburbs?"

"It's a cop-out. What's the use of moving to a great city if we don't live in it and open our children and ourselves to new experiences?"

James heard his mother's voice, barely under control.

"Moving is hard enough after seventeen years without such a drastic change," she said slowly, menacingly. "The suburbs would have been easier for the kids, especially James. Now it's like a kick in the pants."

Hearing his name James stood up and climbed a few more steps. He was poised to run, one hand on the wide mahogany banister.

His father was the one who exploded first.

"All I'm trying to do is something better for my family and I'm accused of brutalizing my own children!" he cried, striding from the living room to the front door.

"Alan!" called his mother.

James ran upstairs. He heard his mother's footsteps and then he heard the front door slam.

James's room had high ceilings, a working fireplace with a white marble mantle, and big bay windows facing the street. It did not feel like his room and he didn't like it. All it had was his sleeping bag, knapsack, a few school books, and a new red telephone on the floor. What he particularly didn't like was a plaster garland of roses that circled the spot on the ceiling where a chandelier once hung. They should have given this room to his sister.

His mother had been too upset to make dinner and said they could boil their own frankfurters on the

Coleman stove if they wanted to. James had retreated to his room and was eating a candy bar instead. He didn't feel much like eating, either.

He took a blue bandana handkerchief from the pocket of his jeans and pulled the phone toward him. He wrapped the handkerchief around the mouthpiece and dialed the long distance number to Oregon.

Lacey's mother answered.

"May I please speak to a Miss Lacey Stevens?" said James, talking from his throat like a gangster.

"She's not at home."

His fake voice dissolved.

"She's *not*?" he asked in dismay. "You sure?"

"This is her mother. Who is *this*?"

James went back to the voice.

"This is the Official Nationwide Polling Service. We're taking a survey of teenage reaction to the international monetary crisis."

"I'm sure she's not interested."

"Parents often do not know what their children's true interest is," said James. "When will she be home?"

"Listen," Lacey's mother sounded annoyed, "who is this, anyway? What do you want?"

James gave the phone a wide fake grin and very gently lowered the receiver, taking off the blue bandana to wipe his damp forehead.

30.

At school the next day they sent him to the Guidance Office.

The Guidance Office was painted mint green and featured a poster on the wall which said "Career Opportunities in Horticulture" with an airbrush painting of a woman from 1940, wearing her hair in a snood and holding a potted plant.

"I'm supposed to see Mr. Hartridge," he told the paunchy middle-aged man who sat at the desk.

"I'm Mr. Hartridge," said the man. "Have a seat."

James sat on the edge of a chair in front of the desk. "I'm James Hunter. What am I supposed to do?"

The guidance counselor picked up some files.

"Hunter, James. Let's see." He riffled through the files. "I can't seem to find you."

"I'm new. From Oregon."

"Ah," Mr. Hartridge raised his eyebrows and put down the files, "that must be it."

"What?"

"They probably want to assign you to the Learning Center for a while."

"What's that?"

"Oh, it's a very nice set-up that gives students a chance to catch up in areas they've fallen behind in," he said with a smile.

"You mean it's for dumb kids."

"No, not at all. There are lots of reasons students have problems in their subjects. In your case it's probably just a change in curriculum."

"We had a great curriculum." James swung the tips of his sneakers against the floor. He felt like he had to fight for the reputation of his old school.

"I don't doubt it," said the man, folding his hands on the desk, "but it was probably different from ours. At the Learning Center you can get special help."

"Special help?" asked James suspiciously.

"We all need help at one time or another. It's nothing to be ashamed of."

"Sure." James stood up and walked toward the door.

"Wait," the counselor called, "let me explain . . ."

"I can't," said James, "I forgot something."

His hand was on the doorknob.

"What did you forget?" asked the counselor, standing up behind his desk.

"I forgot my little sister. I left her in an all-night movie," said James, talking fast and opening the door, "and she can't speak English!"

He stepped out into the hall. He looked in both directions, turned left, and sprinted for his locker, the exit doors, the street.

The guidance counselor picked up his files, this time with concern.

"Hunter, James," he mumbled, brows furrowed, "Hunter, James . . ." trying to find some notation on his record which would explain why James Hunter had just run away.

31.

James's knapsack was packed. He had decided he would leave at dawn.

"Kathy's at the library? Well, just say her brother called. James. Just to say hello. I mean goodbye. Well, both, really."

James was holding the phone and pacing back and forth in his room. He hung up and dialed another number. The Weather Service. But it only told him the weather for Boston and vicinity—continued cold and maybe snow.

"What about the rest of the country?" he asked the recording. "What about Oregon?"

He replaced the receiver and continued to pace. At last he set the phone on the floor and sat down beside it. He would take a bus as far as he could and hitch the rest of the way. Maybe he would get a ride with a trucker. A clear shot to the west. Or maybe somebody rich in a fancy car would be so moved by James's story of traveling cross-country to be with the woman he loved that they'd buy him an airline ticket for the rest of the way.

He couldn't wait for the night to be over so he could escape the forces that held him—his parents, moving, the guidance counselor, school . . .

He slept in his clothes that night so that when the alarm went off at 5:00 A.M. he would be ready to move.

At the last moment he decided to say goodbye to Sandy.

He came into her room dressed for travel—knapsack on his back, sleeping bag tied to it, camera around his neck, hunting knife in his belt, mess kit dangling.

"Does Lacey know you're coming?" Sandy asked, sitting up in her sleeping bag and rubbing her eyes. Her long hair was loose and mussed from sleep and she didn't look much like a football player in her baby-blue nightgown.

"Not yet. I'll call her along the way."

Cold pink light fell through Sandy's bare room. At one time it had been the maid's quarters. The slanted ceiling and dormer windows would someday look sweet with flowered wallpaper, sports posters, and a small brass bed. But now the winter light picked up dust motes on the floor and water stains in the old plaster.

"But what'll you and Lacey do?" Sandy asked.

"I've said too much already," said James, tucking in his shirt.

"You don't trust me."

"I do. But I don't trust *Them*."

"I'll never tell," Sandy promised.

"They have their ways."

Sandy raised her right hand. "I swear on my oath."

"What oath?"

"My sacred oath. That I'll never squeal. No matter what they do to me. No matter if they won't sign permission for football ever again. I'll become a free agent."

"Okay," said James, squatting beside her. The mess kit clanked on the floor. "My plan is, I'll get Lacey and we'll go and live in Canada."

"How come Canada?"

"People always hide out in Canada. Like the guys who were against the Vietnam War."

"Oh, yeah," Sandy said with a yawn, "we had it in Social Studies."

"Besides, you can live off the land in Canada. You can build your own log cabin and hunt and fish, like in the *Whole Earth Catalogue*."

"Can I come and visit?" Sandy asked.

"Sure. You can stay in the guest room. Of the log cabin."

"Thanks. Hey, James?" Sandy crawled out of the sleeping bag and opened the closet. It was empty except for a pair of jeans, a laundry bag, and a deflated volleyball.

"Take this old volleyball of mine," she said, tossing it to him.

"Thanks, Sandy," he said, holding it in his hands, "but I don't know if I'll be playing much volleyball on the road."

"There's thirty-seven dollars stuck in the lining," Sandy said. "From my paper route."

"Hey, thanks," James brightened, taking out the folded money. "I'll buy a bus ticket for as far as this'll take me."

"It'll give you a quick getaway."

"They won't know right away 'cause it's Saturday," said James. "They'll just think I'm sleeping late."

"I'll never tell," Sandy vowed.

"I'll write when I get the log cabin guest room finished."

Sandy walked him to the door of her room. A small hallway window of stained glass filtered the light coming down the stairs in bands of yellow and red. The house seemed peaceful and quiet.

"Good luck, James," Sandy sniffed and brushed her nose with the back of her hand. Her hair was splayed around her shoulders. "Just stay away from the preverts."

James punched her gently on the arm. "Give 'em hell, kid," he said, turning quickly down the steps, trying to swallow the tightness which had suddenly gripped him in the throat.

32

Sandy fell asleep and woke three hours later. She put on sweatshirt and jeans, pulled her hair back in a ponytail, being too lazy to braid it, and went down to the living room to throw a practice whiffle ball against the wall.

The living room now had two folding chairs which were borrowed from her father's college. When her parents came downstairs, still wearing bathrobes, they each sat in a chair in the middle of the empty room. Her father was going over some bills, her mother reading the paper.

"When do we have breakfast?" Sandy asked. "I'm starving."

"When your brother James wakes up," answered her mother, "and decides to join us."

"Oh," said Sandy too hastily, "that's okay. He probably needs his rest."

Her parents looked over at each other.

"Since when are you so concerned with James getting his rest?" her mother asked.

Sandy continued to throw the ball against the wall.

"I do not feel free to comment on that comment," she said.

"Sandy, what's going on?" Her father had removed his reading glasses.

"Nothing," she said.

"I'm going up to see." Her mother stood, tightened the belt of her bathrobe, and walked up the stairs. The last time Sandy had acted guilty and tried to protect her brother was when they had both smashed a four-hundred-dollar glass coffee-table while playing hardball in the den, and James was hiding in his room, trying to glue the pieces back together before his parents found out.

The sound of Sandy's whiffle ball cracking rhythmically against the wall continued. Her father put down his papers. "What's he done that you're not telling us?"

Before Sandy could answer her mother appeared at the foot of the steps.

"He's gone," she said.

"What do you mean? He's not in his room?"

"He's gone. He's taken his knapsack and bedroll. Even his camera."

Her voice was wavering at the edge of tears. Her eyes were bewildered, worried. Sandy tried to edge out of the room.

"Sandy!" ordered her father, "you get back here. This is a family emergency and you're part of it."

Sandy slunk back into the room and sat cross-legged on the floor with her arms folded and lips pressed tightly together.

Her parents got down on their hands and knees in front of her, the better to confront her face to face.

"Out with it," said her father.

"Where's James?"

Sandy spoke through tightened lips. "I'm not at liberty to reveal my brother's whereabouts," she said.

"Sandy, if you know where he's gone you have a moral obligation to help us—so we can help *him*."

"What if he doesn't need your help?" Sandy said in a regular voice.

"He needs it, dear," said her mother, "whether he thinks he wants it right now or not. If you know anything at all you've got to tell us."

Her lips were sealed again.

"I can't," she said from her throat, like a ventriloquist.

"Why not?" demanded her father.

Sandy kept her eyes on the ceiling, as if to even look at her inquisitors would give something away.

"I took a sacred oath I wouldn't. And a *sacred* oath beats a *moral* obligation."

Her father slapped his hand against the floor. His face was growing red from the effort of staying on all fours. "For Heaven's sake!" he said, "we're not playing poker."

Her mother turned to him.

"If you were James and felt rotten, where would you go?"

"Back home?"

"That seems awfully far. How about his big sister?"

"I'll call Kathy!" said her father, as both parents struggled to stand up and get to the phone.

33.

James used the $37 plus $13 of his own money to buy a bus ticket to Canton, Ohio. He had $21 left.

He didn't realize that he had booked a ride going south and then west, and he wound up on a bus bound for New York City and then Pittsburgh. He sat back against a gray velveteen seat and watched Connecticut slip past. The morning bus was not crowded. In front of him sat a girl wearing a Montreal Canadien's team jacket. James stared at the emblem, thinking about how it would be for him and Lacey high up in the Canadian Rockies . . .

He saw the log cabin surrounded by pine trees at the foot of a ragged, snow-covered mountain. It would be winter with snow piled up to the window, but Lacey would keep the window boxes miraculously filled with homey red geraniums.

He saw a figure approach on a large chestnut horse that snorted steam from its nostrils. The rider was himself—James Hunter, dressed as a Royal Canadian Mountie in jodphurs and military jacket, wearing

General MacArthur's hat and clenching a corncob pipe between his teeth. He wore dark glasses as well. And instead of a rifle he held a hockey stick.

The horse and rider approached the cabin. The door flew open and two huskies raced out, barking their welcome. From inside came the smell of corn bread baking, and coffee, and maybe a roast beef, as Lacey Stevens rushed from the doorway, wearing a long pioneer dress and bonnet.

"I have returned!" said James from atop the horse.

"How was your day, my hero?" she asked, grasping the bridle of the stomping horse, gazing up at James with bright eyes.

"I captured the infamous Bobby Orr, my love," he replied, brandishing the hockey stick . . .

When Kathy heard the news of James's disappearance, she got a ride with a friend and made it home in two hours. She appeared at the door wearing a heavy blue wool cape over a turtleneck with corduroy overalls tucked into high boots. A bright plaid scarf hung around her neck and she was carrying a grocery bag.

Her parents were going out as she came in.

"Get a bite to eat while you're out," she told them, unwrapping that scarf. "Take your time. Rushing isn't going to help."

"How can we eat?" said her mother, pulling on a coat. "Our son has run away." They were going to the police station.

"Listen, Mom," Kathy said, "James is a bright kid. He's not going to get himself in trouble. He was probably just upset."

"We'll be all right," her father said, putting an arm around his wife. "You try and crack Sandy."

"You make her sound like a criminal," said her mother. "She's just a kid trying to do what's right."

"It was just a little joke."

"How can you joke," asked her mother, the strain of the past few hours already showing in her face, "when our son has run away?"

"Hey, you guys, relax," Kathy said, "we don't know for sure he's run away." She herded them toward the front door. "Don't you worry about Sandy. I'll have a good talk with her."

She kissed her mother on the cheek and her parents left the house.

"Sandy!" she called up the steps. "It's me. Kathy."

She took off her cape and went into the living room where she placed the paper bag on one of the chairs. She took out two quarts of ice cream, a bottle of chocolate syrup, a jar of pecans, a squirt can of whipped topping, and a packet of plastic spoons and plates.

"Hiya, Sis," said Sandy, appearing at the doorway. "Welcome to Boston."

She saw the ice cream. "What's that?"

"Just some ice cream and syrup and stuff."

"What kind?"

"Regular coffee for me. Raspberry-Royal-Swirl-Ripple for you. And sundae toppings for whoever wants it."

Sandy put her hands in her pockets. "It's a bribe."

"Have I ever tried to trick you before?" Kathy asked.

"Well. Not since I was a gullible kid."

Kathy was tearing the plastic packet of spoons open with her teeth. "That was games, though, right?" she said. "This is not games."

Sandy's eyes were on the ice cream.

"I don't have to break my sacred oath if I eat some of that, do I?"

"No," Kathy assured her, "you have *my* sacred oath on that."

Sandy rushed for the ice cream, and they both began to pile it on their plates. Sandy squirted a small mountain of whipped topping over her ice cream, rapturously moving the nozzle around in an ascending spiral, watching the cream pile up in delicate layers.

"I'm glad you understand about things being sacred, Kathy," she said.

"I think I do," Kathy said, spooning some plain coffee ice cream and trying to sound casual. "I also know you'd want to help James if you thought he really needed it."

"Sure I would. But what if he doesn't want our help? What if he just wants to run away?"

"The trouble is, Sandy, he's never done it before. He might not be very good at it."

"What do you have to be good at?"

"Well," said Kathy, licking her spoon, "you've got to take care of yourself. Protect yourself. From police. From strangers who might be mean or even dangerous. People he doesn't know, with questions and rules he doesn't understand. He might get hurt, in lots of ways, if we don't find him."

They ate in silence. Sandy became absorbed in creating a river of chocolate down the side of her whipped cream mountain. She watched the syrup slide slowly down and over the side of the plate, where she caught it with her spoon.

"Well, I can't really tell what I promised not to tell," she told her sister at last, "but I guess I can give you a hint."

"Hints are fair."

"Okay, here's a hint. A certain boy I know has this plan to go back to where he used to live and get this certain girl he used to go with and take her to Canada with him and they'd build a log cabin in the woods and hunt and fish and sometime I could go visit him and Lacey when he builds the guest room of the log cabin."

She stopped and looked at Kathy.

"Thank you very much, Sandy," Kathy said, sticking her spoon in the ice cream and starting to stand up. "I honestly feel you did the right thing to give me the hint."

"I didn't break my sacred oath?"

"No. I think in the best sense, you kept it."

"What do we do now?" Sandy asked her sister.

She was standing now, moving toward the hallway phone. "Try to find James," she said.

34.

The bus stopped at an institutionalized highway restaurant on the Interstate somewhere in Ohio. It was
10:00 A.M.

"Remember, folks," said the driver as they climbed
off, "ten minutes. Bus pulls out in ten minutes."

James had been riding all day and all night,
through Pennsylvania farmland, small towns, in-
dustrial cities. He had watched out the window as
long as he could and had dozed fitfully in his seat. He
had bought comic books at a stop in the middle of the
night and had read them twice. He ate two apples and
a candy bar from his knapsack, and gradually his
body became numb to the hunger and strain of sitting
up. He was aware of only one sensation—heading
west.

He stepped off the bus and ran ahead of the old
people and mothers with kids into the vestibule of the
restaurant where they had hot-drink machines and
souvenir postcards of Ohio.

He slipped into a phone booth and dialed Lacey's

number, cupping his hand over the receiver in case he had to disguise his voice. He closed the door of the booth to shut out the sounds of wailing babies and the smell of rancid hamburgers.

"I'd like to make a person-to-person call to Miss Lacey Stevens with charges reversed," he said.

"Who is the call from?" asked the operator.

"Uh—it's from—uh—Mr. MacArthur. Mr. Douglas MacArthur."

The phone rang on the other side of the continent and Lacey answered.

"Hello?"

"I have a collect call for Miss Lacey Stevens from Mr. MacArthur," the operator said.

"Mr. Who?"

"Lacey! It's me, James!" he cried.

"Will you accept the call?"

"Yes," said Lacey. Then, "James? Who's Mr. MacArthur?"

"You know, General MacArthur, the guy we studied in World War II history. The guy who said, 'I shall return.' Well, I'm just like him, just like I said I'd be. 'I shall return.' Well, here I come. Returning."

"You were going to come in the spring."

"I couldn't wait," said James, *imagining the spring, and he and Lacey running toward each other, in slow motion, from opposite ends of a field filled with swaying grass.*

"James," said Lacey, "you said spring. I'm awfully busy now."

"With school you mean?"

"Partly."

"What else?"

She paused. "You remember your friend, Rip Lindeman? The halfback?"

"Sure!" said James, smiling in the phone booth. "How is ole buddy Rip?"

"Oh James—" her voice became all sweet and breathless, "he's *heavenly*."

Then James saw the end of the fantasy—him and Lacey approaching each other in the field and her running right past him, into the arms of Rip Lindeman, as James stumbled over into a ditch.

"We couldn't help it, James," Lacey went on. "It just *happened* to us. It was magic."

The bus driver appeared at the doorway of the vestibule.

"It happened?" James repeated softly.

"On board, everybody," called the driver.

James looked at the doorway of the restaurant where passengers were heading back toward the bus. His attention came back to the phone booth, to Lacey's presence, her breath, her aliveness on the other end of the line.

She was saying something more, but James was already hanging up the phone. Click. Disconnection. The phone hung there dead, ready for the next person to try to call someone they loved from this godforsaken strip of highway. James slid the door of the phone booth open and ran to the bus, pushing ahead of other passengers, squeezing down the aisle to take his knapsack from the rack over his seat.

"Hey, kid," said the driver, as he made his way out, "you don't get off here."

"Yes I do," said James, scrambling down the steps.

The silver door of the big bus wheezed shut. The bus backed up and turned out of the parking lot and onto the highway, leaving James alone in a cloud of exhaust.

He began to walk. He walked along the highway

where the ground was frozen, although cars were passing dangerously close. When he came to an exit ramp he followed it up over a small bridge and stood looking down at the road stretching west.

Cars zoomed beneath him, heading for important destinations. What would be his? He had left his first home in Oregon and his second home in Boston. He had been betrayed by the only person in the world he trusted. Betrayed for a fast-talking jock. The only facts he could rely on now were the feel of his hiking boots against the concrete of the bridge, the knapsack pulling heavily on his shoulders, the cramps of hunger in his belly, and the resounding knowledge that he was alone.

Alone and heading for that region of wilderness where men could start all over again. Where men were forced to make their own lives. North. To Canada.

35.

The HiSpot Diner was open and James sat in a booth eating a cheeseburger and chocolate malted for breakfast. It was a splurge, but he figured he needed it now that he was heading into the frozen wasteland.

"Isn't it cold to be camping out?" asked the waitress.

"It's for my Boy Scout Merit Badge," James said sweetly. "Winter survival."

He bought some candy bars on the way out and walked through the town to a crossroads where he saw a sign indicating Route 45 North. He started to walk backward, thumb out. The sky was gray but seemed to be holding. They were still predicting a storm. Cars and pickup trucks passed slowly on the two-lane road and he flashed them the grin but none stopped.

He was about to turn and start walking when he saw a female hitchhiker coming toward him on the road.

She was taller than he, wearing a thrift-shop fur coat over jeans and high leather boots. She wore a stocking cap, had a flight bag over her shoulder, and carried a sketchpad. A nylon knapsack was strapped over the fur coat. James did not want her stealing his hitching turf, so he hurried further up the road. She was running after him.

"Hey!" she called.

"No!" said James over his shoulder.

"You've got it all wrong!"

James turned to face her but kept moving backwards, mess kit clanking against his leg.

"I was here before you," he called.

"Big deal. Want to *stay* here or get moving and get a ride?"

James kept walking backwards and tripped. He fell down in a heap, his knapsack and camping gear tangled around him. He let himself sit there on the road for a moment because the exhaustion of his twenty-eight-hour adventure had just swept over him.

The young woman came up to him and squatted down on the road. She was older than he.

"I'm going to Canada," he said, breathing hard.

He saw she was pretty, with dark hair stuck under a green stocking cap.

"It's not too cool to advertise it," she said, "I mean if you happen to be underage by any chance."

"I happen to be a hockey fan," said James belligerently, "who is on his way to Canada to see the Canadiens and Maple Leafs play, as they've always been my favorite teams and hockey's my favorite sport except for basketball, and then I'm a Trail Blazers fan."

"You don't have to tell me your life story," said the hitchhiker, appraising him, "I just want to help."

"Why?"

"People on the road help each other."

"How?"

"Right now I can help you get a ride a lot quicker if we team up."

"Why?"

"Well, the sexist fact is a guy has a better chance of getting a ride if he's with a girl, and equally sexist, a girl won't be hassled as much with a guy along."

James struggled to get up under the weight of his gear.

"Oh," he said.

"On top of which we seem to be going in the same approximate direction, more or less."

"What do I do?" asked James.

"Standing up would help, for a start." She stood, extended her hands, and pulled James to his feet. He reached up nervously to smooth the hair over his ear.

"Thanks," he said.

"I'm Robin. We partners?"

"I guess," he said. "I'm James. Sure."

Robin knew how to exploit the "sexist facts" of life to get a ride. She told James to hide in the bushes while she walked up to the side of the blacktop road. She took off the green stocking cap and stuffed it in her pocket, shaking out a mane of wavy black hair. She rolled her jeans to just below the tops of her boots, opened her fur coat and took a stance with one leg thrust forward and thumb out. With the other hand she made a victory sign in the shape of a fist which James, peering out between the bushes, returned.

She turned on a smile and within thirty seconds a new white car had pulled over to the side of the road. She ran for it, opened the front door, put two fingers in her mouth, and whistled loud and strong. James came thrashing out of the underbrush and ran for the open door, his cooking kit and knapsack bouncing. He plunged into the back seat while Robin got in the front and slammed the door.

The driver, about thirty, was wearing a doubleknit suit and had short hair. Sheafs of price lists and machine parts slid along the dashboard as he pulled out onto the road. He was obviously a salesman making the rounds.

He looked back at James.

"Who the hell's *he*?" the driver said.

"My brother," answered Robin.

The driver's eyes rolled up to heaven. "Her brother," he said.

Robin turned back to James and winked.

They picked up Route 62 heading east. Robin was going to Vermont and James figured that Vermont was as good a gateway to Canada as anyplace. From there he could shoot north to Montreal.

It was a rented car, covered with plush white velvet inside with soft white vinyl seats. James stretched out in back. He could watch bare tops of trees going by through the windows and listen to the schmaltzy music station the salesman played. At least it was music. He dozed.

"Yes," Robin was saying as James awoke, eighty miles later, "I want to become a forest ranger."

James sat up. He saw the salesman's arm lying along the back seat, his fingers stretching toward Robin, who had wedged herself against the door, knees drawn up.

"Never heard of a girl forest ranger before," the driver said. "What do you have to do to be one?"

Robin glanced back at James and grimaced. He realized this conversation had been going on for some time.

"Well, aside from a college degree, you have to have archery, marksmanship, animal training, and karate," Robin said.

But the driver was not listening to her fantastic claims.

"Aw, c'mon," he said, "why don't we stop at a nice motel. We could all have dinner and then your brother could go watch TV and you and me could have a few laughs."

Robin sat up now, tense. She looked back at James.

"No—listen—" she said, "we really can't. *Can* we, Horace?"

"No way, Sis," said James, "I—uh—I haven't had my injection yet today. We better find the nearest hospital."

The driver peered at James through the rearview mirror.

"Injection for what?"

"My disease."

"Disease? What disease?"

"It's very rare," said Robin, "but it runs in our family."

"She has it too," added James, "but she only has to have her injection every *other* day, instead of *every* day like me."

"Oh, Horace, thank Heaven you remembered!" Robin said.

She turned toward the driver, whose fingers had begun to withdraw along the back of the seat.

"If the symptoms come over him, don't be alarmed," she said. "Just let us out where it's most convenient."

"Symptoms?" said the driver, looking in the rearview mirror again. "What symptoms?"

James made the "Beaver Face" and let out a bloodcurdling screech. *"Aaaarrggll-awwggglll-iggggghhh!"*

The car skidded to a halt at the side of the road.

36.

James was beginning to understand the rules of the road. By afternoon he and Robin were on Route 6 in Pennsylvania, riding the back of a red pickup truck along with a load of two-by-fours. They huddled beneath some old oil-stained blankets against the cab of the truck, trying to keep out of the stream of wind. It was cold out in the open and they pulled their caps down over their foreheads and kept their hands in their pockets.

James was also finding it easy to confess everything to Robin.

"It wasn't hardly a couple of weeks," he was saying loudly, over the noise of the truck, "and Lacey's going with this guy Rip. The great jock hero . . ."

"I know the type," Robin said. "*Both* types."

Some metal object was rolling back and forth along the serrated floor of the truck. The load of wood kept shifting as they rounded curves.

"So what do you do?" James asked.

Robin pretended to wet one finger of her gloved hand on her tongue and make a mark in the air.

"Chalk it up," she said.

"That's what I'm trying to do," said James, squinting against the cold. "Just go to Canada. Chalk up the rest."

"You have any friends there? In Canada?"

"Not yet."

"That can be rough," Robin said.

"Not any more than this rotten new school I had to go to," said James.

They were riding through a small town with white houses fronting a wide street. It reminded James of home. Some kids his age were hanging around on a corner, holding schoolbooks and horsing around. The pickup truck turned a corner and continued out of town. A souped-up Dodge came screeching by on the right, leaving rubber and a trail of rock music. James watched with envy.

"All schools are bummers at first," Robin said. "My first semester at college I kept throwing up all the time."

"What did you do about it?" asked James.

"I just hung in there."

"It sounds like prison."

"They call it 'higher education,'" Robin said.

The truck let them off near Towanda, Pennsylvania. According to Robin's worn *Road Atlas* they had traveled almost three hundred miles from where they had met in Ohio. She said for a day's hitching it was pretty good.

They stood at the side of the road in the twilight.

"What do we do now?" asked James.

"Find someplace to sleep," said Robin, walking confidently ahead.

He followed, feeling the cold against his face. He wondered if she were going to knock on a farmer's door and ask if they could spend the night. Like brother and sister, Hansel and Gretel, lost. Or would they check into a motel? Try to get another ride and sleep in a car? He couldn't think. He was too hungry and cold.

"There it is," Robin said, pointing to a barn on a hill silhouetted against the darkening sky. "Come on." She began to climb the shoulder of the road.

The boards of the barn were weathered gray, with not a speck of paint left on them. The big front doors had been locked with a motorcycle chain long rusted over, but side windows were broken and James and Robin managed to climb inside.

"How do you find places like this?" asked James when they stood in the center of the deserted barn.

"You go out on the road enough, you develop an instinct. Like that salesman could find a cheap motel. Easy. You sniff it out."

They discovered other people had already sniffed out this particular place, as there was a fire site already dug in the dirt floor, orange crates to sit on, and beer cans and cigarette stubs scattered nearby.

They took off their knapsacks.

"Hey, look!" called James. In one of the old stalls was a pile of wood all cut for a fire.

"We've got good hosts," Robin said, "whoever they are."

James pulled off a log and a mouse ran out of the woodpile.

"There's one," he said.

Robin took two oranges and a half-loaf of hard

bread from her knapsack. She unwrapped a piece of cheese.

"Dinner for two," she said.

James handed her a candy bar from his pocket.

"And dessert!"

"Do you just drop out of college when you go on the road?" he asked.

"Just for a little while. Then I drop back in. Like this time."

"Where've you been?" asked James. He was unconsciously making a fire the way his father did—three logs in the shape of an A, kindling in the center.

"Chicago Art Institute," Robin said. "I wanted to look at a painting. *Clouds*. This far-out beautiful lady did it. Georgia O'Keeffe."

James took a waterproof matchbox from his pocket. He was glad he'd remembered to bring it.

"You went all the way just to look at a picture?" he said.

"*Just*? Hey. You better believe it was worth it. You don't just *see* a painting like that. It shows you *how* to see."

She watched as he touched the match to his pile of straw and twigs. The flame was steady. Carefully, he added more wood.

"I just look around, I guess," said James.

"Don't give me that," answered Robin. "You have a camera."

"I used to take pictures."

"You don't any more?"

"I dunno."

"Come off it," Robin said. "Take a picture of me."

James looked at her from where he was kneeling at the fire. It was going well now, casting orange light around them, showing warmly on Robin's face and in a tiny jumping reflection on a piece of window glass left on the far side of the barn. Outside it was black.

James rose, brushed straw from his knees, and picked up his knapsack. Robin was standing with her coat draped off one shoulder, thumb out, pretending to be the seductive hitchhiker. James opened his camera case as she took another pose, this one with hands clasped behind her head, moistening her lips like a model.

"Come on, Ace Photographer," she said, "I'm ready."

James had the camera around his neck. He walked toward her.

"Well?" she said. "Aren't you going to check the light?"

But James had both hands on her shoulders and was rushing forward as if to tackle and kiss her at the same time. She stepped back, lost her balance, and they both tumbled to the floor of the barn.

Robin pushed him off gently. "Did you really want to do that, James?" she said.

"Well, I thought —I thought I was supposed to—" he said, standing up, fixing the hair over his ear. "I thought you wanted—"

"You thought you should do a macho number?" Robin confronted him while still sitting on the floor. "James. Don't ever do anything just because you think you're supposed to. Or you think somebody else thinks you're supposed to."

"I'm sorry," said James. "I guess I messed everything up."

"Spare me the suds, James," Robin said, standing up. "You're better than that."

James just stared at the ground. "I dunno," he said.

"Well, I *do*," said Robin. She sat down on an orange crate next to the food and took out a Swiss Army knife. "Tomorrow you can use your camera. And your head."

37.

The police told James's parents there were a lot of runaway kids in Massachusetts and until they filed a Missing Persons report or brought criminal charges against their son as a "stubborn child," there was nothing the police could do. They were advised to go home and wait for word from James, who would probably call when he ran out of money.

The furniture arrived that day from Oregon but James's mother was too upset from worrying to try to unpack. His father went back and forth between college and home, waiting for a call from James and trying to comfort his wife

The downstairs was filled with boxes and pieces of furniture left in unlikely places like the kitchen and hall. The family decided to leave it until the next day. Kathy said she would stay until James came home and bedded down in his room.

But neither parent could sleep. At one o'clock in the

morning they both went downstairs in their bathrobes.

James's mother snapped on the overhead bulb. The room was crossed with angular shadows where light hit stacks of boxes and cartons. It seemed impossible that out of the brown cardboard would come the objects and accoutrements that create a home. At this hour on a winter night, in a strange city, their son missing, they scarcely felt they were setting up house. They needed something to do to keep from panicking.

"Moving therapy," she said kneeling down to rip open a carton marked "China."

"I feel like a hijacker doing this in the middle of the night," said her husband, lifting an armchair.

"It's better than lying in bed and not sleeping." She unfolded newspaper from around a china teapot. "Besides, if James shows up and it looks more like a home, maybe he'll feel . . . more at home. If he comes home."

The teapot slipped from her hand and shattered on the floor. It was part of a set which had been her mother's—hand-painted with a pattern of wildflowers. She began to cry.

Her husband set down the chair and put his arm around her. He led her to the couch which was standing in the middle of the room.

"Hey, Meg," he said softly.

"The worst part is we can't *do* anything," she sobbed, reaching into her bathrobe for a tissue.

"Darling, the police said the best we could do is stay right here. We'll be here then when James *does* come home."

"Maybe it's *not* a home," she said, "having the furniture doesn't make it one."

"What are you talking about?"

"Us."

"What about us?"

James's mother stood up, thrusting the tissue back into the pocket of her terrycloth robe. She bent over to pick up one side of the couch.

"If we aren't right anymore, then there isn't any family," she said.

"Is something wrong with us?" Her husband picked up his side of the couch.

"We've just been going through the motions lately. We fight. We take each other for granted—like so much furniture."

"That's crazy, Meg," said her husband, "I love you."

"When's the last time you told me?"

They angled the couch over toward the window. The bare white walls resounded with their footsteps and the squeak of furniture legs against the hardwood floor.

"I tell you lots of times."

"When's the last?"

They stared at each other across the length of sofa.

"If you have to rack your brain it proves my point," she said.

Her husband put down his side of the couch as she did the same.

"I'm sorry, Meg," he told her.

"So am I. It's crucial to me. To know you love me."

"But you *know* I do."

"I'd like to be reminded sometimes, instead of just assuming it."

Alan sat down on the sofa and his wife came around to sit beside him, but he drew her onto his lap and kissed her.

"If I take you for granted, it's the way I take food

and water for granted. Essential things. That I couldn't live without—you most of all."

"Show me," said his wife.

And he kissed her, again.

38.

By the afternoon of the third day, James and Robin had made it to Kingston, New York.

"We've been lucky with the weather," Robin said. "Hasn't been that cold."

It was sunny that day and they could almost smell a wetness like spring in the woods, but it was just last week's melting snow. They had stopped in a grocery outside the town to buy lunch and were walking the road that ran just below the New York State Thruway.

"You thumbed all the way from Vermont to California last year?" asked James. His camera hung around his neck. Robin carried the brown grocery bag.

"It wasn't a direct trip," she said. "I stopped in Milwaukee to see my Mom and her new husband, then in Alburquerque to visit my Dad and his new wife. So I had a lot of momentum going. Also during the holidays, people are full of one type of spirit or another and it's no sweat at all getting rides."

"Stay there," said James, focusing the camera. Robin smiled back at him, easy and natural this time, and he took the shot. "You see the Rose Bowl?" he asked, catching up with her.

"Not the game," Robin said, "I don't dig people knocking each other around. I caught the Parade, which was kind of a groove, but the main thing was the museum there had just got itself more than three hundred Goyas."

"Is he another artist?"

"Is Muhammad Ali just another boxer? Hey—look!" Robin pointed to a road sign that said "Picnic Table" with a drawing of one on it. "Our table is ready!"

They ran ahead. Set in a little turnout of the road they found a redwood picnic table with a trash barrel and barbecue grill. Behind it were woods.

They put their gear on the table and started unloading groceries.

"It's such a beautiful day," Robin said. "Want to get high before lunch?"

James looked up at her. He wasn't sure what she had in mind.

"Great idea," he said.

Robin sat cross-legged on top of the table and swept off dried catkins which had fallen from overhanging trees. James climbed up beside her.

"Ready?" she asked.

"For anything," replied James.

Robin fluffed her hair out around her shoulders, closed her eyes, and took a quick suck of air as if she were inhaling a joint. But there was no joint. James watched in astonishment as she did it again; this time a calm happy look came over her face.

"Try it," she said, "this stuff is really good."

"What is it?"

"Air."

"Oh."

"It's a natural high," Robin said. "Doesn't mess up your head or your lungs."

She closed her eyes again. James did the same and began to breath deeply, slowly. He was amazed to feel his body easing up. He could feel the tiredness in it, but even that felt good. Soon the gray swirling inside his eyelids subsided and he saw a calm field of blue. He smiled and let himself roll sideways on the table. Robin, sensing him, rolled over as well, and they opened their eyes and laughed, rolling onto their sides like two weighted toys.

Robin stood up on the seat of the table.

"That gives you an appetite," she said, jumping down. "Let's eat."

She pulled out a loaf of sprouted-wheat bread, packaged bologna, and her knife, and began making sandwiches.

"You remind me of my sister Kathy," James said, striding the bench. He leaned his elbows on the table and focused the camera.

"How?" asked Robin, licking mustard from her knuckle. "Looks or deeds?"

James took the shot.

"She does things sort of like the way you make bologna sandwiches," he said, lowering the camera. "No horsing around."

"Thanks," Robin said, "I like that. You know what else?"

"What?"

"I think Kathy's lucky. I don't have any sisters or brothers."

"You'd make a great sister."

"Well, since we can't be that why don't be we friends? I mean real friends."

"Sure," said James uncertainly.

"Have you ever had a girl for a friend before?" Robin asked. She was wiping the mustard from her knife against the inside of a slice of bread.

"I had girlfriends before. Like Lacey."

"I don't mean girlfriend. I mean a friend who's a girl."

"I guess not."

"It's a nice thing. For a guy and a girl to be friends. Not lovers, but friends. Sometimes they can help each other out, talk to each other, better than with friends of the same sex. They don't have to do any numbers to impress each other. They can relax. And know they can count on each other."

Robin tore off a piece of brown paper from the bag and placed James's sandwich on it, in front of him.

"Could I be your friend that way, Robin?" he asked.

"You're on," she said, winking at him and extending her hand. They shook on it.

James bit into his bologna sandwich and stared into the woods, *imagining himself and Robin dressed in feathered caps, leather tunics and leggings, pulling back on heavy bows as they knelt back to back, firing arrows at the enemy in the woods.*

"*Save your own skin, Robin,*" he shouted. "*We can't stave off the forces of the King and the Sheriff of Nottingham much longer.*"

"*No, Little James,*" she said. "*You sneak off and carry on our noble work.*"

"*Never!*" James declared. "*We'll fight them together till the last arrow!*"

James and Robin stood up, turned to each other, and shook hands while enemy arrows whizzed around them.

"*One for both and both for one!*" they cried, then

*kneeled and drew more arrows from the quivers on
their backs.*

Robin was emptying paper and wrappings into the
trash barrel provided by the New York State Highway
Department.

"Let's get with it," she said. "Groovy afternoon like
this is prime time for travel."

James stuffed the last of the sandwich into his
mouth and stood, just in time to see a handsome
broad-shouldered young man about twenty-one,
carrying a duffel bag and a red-wine flask strapped
across his chest, walking toward him. He had longish
dark hair and a big white smile beneath a black wal-
rus moustache.

"I never could pass up a picnic," he said.

"We were just leaving," said James, dusting off his
hands.

But Robin had stopped dumping trash and was
looking at the young man.

"Rules of the road, James," she said. "We all share."

James sat back down on the bench.

"Groovy afternoon for traveling," he muttered under
his breath.

Robin was now unpacking everything all over
again, laying stuff on the table to make a sandwich
for the stranger.

"Hey, thanks," he said.

"Special of the day," said Robin. "Bologna on
sprouted wheat with mustard. Your genial chef is
Robin."

"I'm Tiger."

"You some kind of boxer or something?" asked
James, glaring at the guy.

"Nope," said Tiger, "just fast on my feet. And at
home in the jungle."

"Hobo jungle? For tramps and like that?"

Tiger took the sandwich from Robin and began to take big bites.

"To me, kid, jungle means anything wild and natural. The sea, the woods, anything they haven't killed with concrete yet."

Robin smiled at him. "I like that," she said.

"This your kid brother?" Tiger asked.

"Just friends," said James.

"We adopted each other on the road," said Robin.

Tiger took his goatskin flask from around his neck, took off the top, and with perfect aim squeezed a stream of red wine into his mouth. He passed it to Robin.

"How about a little of the old grape?" he said. "Goes good with bologna."

She took the flask, squirted it, got some on her lips, and giggled. Looking her in the eye, Tiger reached over and wiped the wine from her mouth.

"That stuff's not bad," Robin said.

James grabbed the flask.

"Not the best vintage," Tiger said, "not the worst. It kind of looks good on you, though."

James tilted his head back, aimed, and squeezed as hard as he could, squirting wine all over his jacket and face.

Tiger and Robin were putting the sandwich things back in her knapsack.

"Does this stuff come off?" asked James.

They turned to see him dripping wine from his collar and chin.

39.

From then on it was different on the road. Robin and Tiger walked ahead of James, talking earnestly, while he dragged along behind like a little kid, kicking stones or picking up sticks and throwing them sideways into the darkness of the woods.

Every time a ride ended, Robin would pull out her *Road Atlas* and show them how far they'd come. He could see their progress up New York State toward Vermont and then the thick red line of Route 91 which he would take, alone, to Canada. He was beginning to think it wouldn't be so bad to be traveling alone. At least he wouldn't have to listen to Tiger's cheerful talk.

"So I got the big degree in Biz Administration," the guy was saying, "stopped off to see the folks in Chicago and sold my wheels. Now I start work."

"I thought businessmen had to have a car," Robin said.

"Not in my business."

"You have to have an office, don't you?"

"Nope. I got myself a gig on a lobster boat in Maine."

Robin laughed. "Outta sight!" she said.

James mimicked her words, mouthing "Outta sight," and making the "Beaver Face" at their backs.

"You know," Robin said, "Vermont's on the way to Maine. If we make it to around Brattleboro tonight, there's a place we can crash. Bunch of people I know have a big old house outside of town."

"A commune?" asked James.

Robin turned to him briefly over her shoulder. "Well, they grow some measly vegetables and wear overalls, so they like to call it a farm." And to Tiger, "I humor 'em."

"They got room for all of us?" called James.

But Robin was preoccupied with Tiger again and didn't hear. Two cars went by.

"*Hey!*" called James, "we gonna walk all the way or get a ride?"

"Sure we are, James. Tiger and I just got to rapping," Robin said.

"Yeah," said James, "I heard."

Robin sent James and Tiger into the bushes, assumed her hitching pose, and in minutes a car had stopped.

The farm in Brattleboro, Vermont consisted of a dilapidated house with a small front porch and graying sides, a few apple trees out back, and a chicken shed.

James, Tiger and Robin sat at a long oak table with four others, two men and two women in their early twenties. The kitchen had been repaneled with weathered barnboard and was well-stocked with big glass jars containing organically-grown grains and spices

from the health food store in town. They had installed
stereo speakers in the kitchen and played Keith Jarrett
as they ate. One of the men was a photographer and
his prints were tacked around the kitchen. One of the
women was a weaver, and her wall hangings hung on
the stairs.

The women wore long skirts and did the cooking.
The men both had full beards and wore flannel shirts
and jeans. James imagined this was the way people
lived in Canada—working outside with their hands,
growing a beard, living simply off the land. He didn't
know this modern farm family lived on welfare, unem-
ployment, and donations from parents.

They ate a thick vegetable stew by candlelight,
with homemade bread, herb tea, and oatmeal cookies
for dessert. Robin and Tiger sat together and talked,
while James watched wax drip and pile up around the
candle nearest him.

"Good meal makes me want to lie down," Tiger said
with his bright smile.

"Jonah?" Robin asked, "Is it cool with you if we
sack out here for the night? We have our sleeping
bags and stuff."

Jonah had a full black beard and soft brown eyes.
He wore red suspenders over his flannel shirt.

"The kid can't stay," he said.

"What are you talking about?"

"He can't spend the night."

A woman named Sarah said, "Jonah, there's room."

"We've been busted once for a crop we were growing," Jonah said quietly, "and we can't afford to get
busted again."

"For what?" Robin said.

"Hiding out an underage kid. Don't you think the
cops are after him yet?"

James had never thought of cops being after him. He felt a chill.

"I'll say he's my brother," Robin said.

"They'll ask for proof."

James stood up. It was below freezing outside.

"It's okay, Robin," he said, trying not to let his voice shake, "I've got my camping gear."

Robin stood as well.

"Jonah, we can't put people out in the night," Sarah said.

"Sorry, Sarah, we can't risk it."

Nobody else said a word. Robin and Tiger looked at each other across the table. James went to the corner, took his jacket from a peg on the wall, and shouldered his knapsack. He shook hands with Tiger. At least this would be the last he'd see of this guy.

"Nice knowing ya," he said, then extended his hand to say goodbye to Robin.

She looked at him and made a decision.

"Sarah," she said, "hack off a piece of the bread for me and James, huh? We tend to get these fits of unbearable hunger."

James smiled. Rules of the road. Robin brushed her hair to one side, dipped under the table, and came up with her flight bag. She took her fur coat from an extra chair.

Sarah, embarrassed, wrapped the rest of the bread in aluminum foil and handed it to Robin who slipped it into her bag. The candles flickered in the draft coming beneath the kitchen door.

Tiger was turned in his seat, watching Robin.

"James and I are friends," she told him. "I want to stick with him till daylight. You get a good night's sleep and I'll fall by in the morning."

Tiger pushed his chair back from the table and stood.

"Oh no you don't," he said. "You'll end up taking the kid to Disneyland and I'll never find you."

This time Robin smiled, and James made a face at the rules of the road.

40.

Outside it was cold and the stars were hidden by clouds.

"Gonna snow," Tiger said, sniffing the air.

"Don't say that," said Robin.

The two walked holding hands in the dark. James went ahead of them, using his flashlight along the pitch dark country road. They had wrapped woolen scarves around their faces but two hundred yards from the house their fingers and toes had become numb.

"We're not going to get anywhere tonight," James said, his voice muffled by the scarf. "No cars."

"What did you say?" Robin called.

He turned. "No cars," he said, pushing the scarf down from his mouth. "There hasn't been a car yet. They couldn't see us in the dark and they wouldn't pick us up anyway."

"Kid's right," Tiger said. "We'd better bag it for tonight."

"But where?" Robin asked. "Damn Jonah and his paranoia."

"Forget it," Tiger said. He looked up at the sky to get his bearings but could not see any stars. "Which way are we going?"

"North," said Robin. "Out of town."

"Well, that's a mistake." Tiger stopped in the road and made an abrupt about-face. "Nothing out there but frozen fields. And tonight we don't want to camp out."

James was thinking maybe they could go back to the farmhouse and tell them it was too cold.

"Let's head back to town," Tiger said. "I bet I know a fine hotel."

"We can't afford a hotel," Robin said.

"Don't worry. This one we can afford."

They trudged back the way they had come. On the way they passed a brightly-lit house from which two dogs came bounding, barking furiously.

"Keep walking," Tiger said. "They'll stop when we're off their territory."

The dogs trotted beside them, barking and snapping. James shined the flashlight in their eyes. When they passed out of the light from the house the dogs turned back.

Robin and Tiger began to sing a song called "Wandering Blues." Their voices sounded fragile in the dark night, breath rising in white vapor. They were singing other folk songs that James knew. He came up on the other side of Robin and she slipped her arm in his. He discovered it was a lot easier to be walking down a dark cold country road when you could link arms and sing.

"There it is," Tiger said. "Our Class-A hotel."

They had walked about two miles back to town and were now standing in front of the town bus terminal. "BUS" it said in blinking lights.

"Won't they kick us out?" asked James as they pulled open the glass doors.

"Not if we don't lie down and fall asleep," Tiger said.

The bus station was warm and practically deserted. The ticket-taker said nothing as they sat down on a long wooden bench in the corner and took off their gear. Their faces were pinched and red from cold.

Robin unzipped her boot and massaged her foot.

James sat down and leaned against a wall.

"See," Tiger told him, "when you know the jungle, you know all the places to hide out. All it takes is experience, kid." Tiger poked him on the arm in a friendly way. James tried to smile.

When the clock on the yellow tiled wall said eleven-thirty, the ticket-taker closed the booth and quietly left the station. They could hear his jeep fire up outside. James dozed. He stood up once to use the men's room and saw Robin and Tiger on the other end of the bench. She was asleep in his arms. The clock said three.

At dawn, buses started rolling in and out of the station. The ticket booth opened up. They bought watery coffee and hot chocolate from a machine and ate the rest of the homemade bread. The clock said seven and outside the steamy windows, they saw buses arriving drenched with snow.

"Gotta get some air," Tiger said, standing up. He gave Robin a kiss on the forehead and headed for the door.

James had circles beneath his eyes. He felt partially revived by the hot chocolate and bread.

"Are you falling for that guy?" he asked.

"I don't know. Maybe."

"You were going to stay with him, right?"

"I like him, James. A lot."

James pushed the hair from his eyes. By now it was so dirty and greasy it stayed where he put it.

"I thought you liked me a lot, too."

"I do. In a different way. You and I are friends. Tiger and I might be lovers."

"You might?"

"But I can't predict the future, James. If it feels right I'll do it. If it's going to be a good thing for both of us."

"Even if it were just for one night?"

"Just because something is temporary doesn't mean it has to be ugly. It can be meaningful."

"I wish I were Tiger," said James.

"Just be yourself. And start making your own decisions."

"What do you mean?"

"Well, decide whether you're really going to go on up to Canada and try to cross the border without getting busted for being underage, and roam around a whole huge country where you don't have a single friend, or whether you're going back to Boston and live with your family and finish school."

She took out her sketchpad and pencil.

"Here," she said, "I'll draw it for you."

She sketched a picture of someone who looked like James with floppy hair over his eyes, wearing a knapsack, right thumb out for hitching, left thumb out as well, pointing in the opposite direction. He was at a crossroads. She put a perplexed look on the face and labeled it "James At Fifteen."

When she finished she looked up at James who smiled, nodding his head.

"Right," he said as she closed the sketchpad. "But Boston's the pits."

"Boston could be a beautiful trip if you give it a chance," Robin said. "A city's like a person. You have to get to know it. And *you've* got the perfect way."

"How?"

"Your camera. Use it as a passport to go places, look at things really hard. You could get a summer job with a newspaper. Find out what the city's all about."

James swirled the last sludge of his hot chocolate around the paper cup.

"Yeah," he said, "and go home and hear my parents crabbing at each other and getting so mad they make each other cry?"

"I heard it for years," Robin said, stretching her legs out in front of her, "till my parents finally split. At least yours stuck together, didn't they?"

"Sure they did. They do, I mean. I think. At least when I was there last. But it seemed bad—you don't think they'd actually—do anything like that, do you?"

He was afraid to use the word "divorce"—like the word "cancer" it seemed to imply awful and inescapable consequences. He imagined if his parents split, each to live in a dark one-room apartment somewhere, he and Sandy would have to support themselves—take to the road and ride boxcars like orphans.

"It happens in the best of families," Robin said.

"What'll I *do*?" said James.

"I wish I could tell you, but I can't," she said, touching his knee with sympathy. "Nobody can. You've got to figure it out for yourself."

Tiger came back to them with a dusting of snow on his shoulders and cap.

"Driver says they're expecting four to six inches," he said. "We'd better get going before we get socked in here."

"Right," Robin said. "One good ride and we're home."

She gathered her things. James sat still on the bench. He was thinking about divorce. Boston. Lacey. School.

"Come on, kid, let's get going," Tiger said.

For a moment he did not reply. He seemed to be staring out the door of the bus station. Out the door and beyond.

"I'm staying here," he said.

Robin looked down at him and bit her lip. She looked over at Tiger and nodded for him to meet her outside.

"Good luck, kid," Tiger said. "Stay fast on your feet." He clapped James on the shoulder.

Robin put one leg up on the bench. She unzipped her boot and pulled out a folded ten-dollar bill. She pressed it into James's hand.

"This will get you a bus ticket to Boston. Or almost as far as the Canadian border," she said. "Your choice."

James felt the money in his hand. "I'll pay you back," he said, "I'll get a job."

He stood up and Robin hugged him. He could smell the wet fur of her coat and some scent of perfume or jasmine soap she managed to maintain, even on the road. Her earrings felt cold against his skin.

"Write me at college and let me know, okay? Which way you go."

James nodded and pulled back. She bent and swiftly picked up her gear and walked toward the door where Tiger waited. At the door she turned and raised her fist to James, and although his eyes were blurred with tears, he managed to return the victory sign.

41.

The snowstorm hit that afternoon and stalled traffic on the highway. The bus ride took ten hours. James slept fitfully, waking from dreams of bad men who picked up hitchhikers and parents who walked out the door carrying suitcases to feel the icy window against his cheek and to look out at blinding snow.

It was dark when the bus pulled into Boston. He was surprised to find that already many of the streets looked familiar to him. Snow was falling in big dry flakes and the city seemed muffled by it. On Commonwealth Avenue two college kids were throwing snowballs under the halo of a street light.

Nobody had ventured to or from the house on Marlborough Street that night. The steps were covered with blank snow. James's boots left wet waffle prints as he climbed to the door and used his key.

Cooking smells came from the kitchen. All their furniture was back and had been set in place. The rooms looked different—lived in, alive. He felt like a spy in

somebody else's home where life was going on without him.

He quietly entered the living room where Sandy
and Kathy sat on the rug playing Scrabble. A fire
blazed behind them.

"Is Y–A–C a word?" Sandy was asking. "Meaning an
ancient beast of burden?"

"We—ell," her sister began.

"Don't let her cheat," said James from the doorway.

"Shut up, James, you're not playing," Sandy said.
Then she stopped. Gasped. And saw her brother.
"*James!*"

She jumped up and threw her arms around his neck.
Kathy, smiling, was standing up too. . . .

His parents came in from the kitchen.

"Oh, thank God!" his mother cried, eyes bright with
tears. James hugged her awkwardly, still wearing the
knapsack and down-filled jacket, which was wine-
stained and wet from snow.

"James," his father hugged him with one strong
arm, "I'm so glad you're home."

Then he stood back and glared at his son.

"Where the hell have you been?" he said.

"I demand full amnesty!" said James.

His mother took a steak from the freezer for him.
After dinner, he went upstairs and slept for fifteen
hours. It was the first time he'd slept in a real bed
since they'd left Oregon.

42.

On his first day back at school James met Mrs. Larsen.

She was the teacher in charge of the Learning Center. She wore jeans and boots to school like the kids. She was in her late twenties and reminded him a lot of Robin except she had short curly hair and wore big glasses.

"James Hunter?" she said. "Welcome to the Learning Center."

She shook his hand. No teacher ever did that before.

The Learning Center was the only room in the school with bright yellow walls and plants in the tall windows. There was a rug on the floor and posters on the wall. One was of a football player with the face of Mary Hartman pasted over his.

Mrs. Larsen and James sat in two chairs near the window. They weren't regular school chairs, but big, comfortable easy chairs. Mrs. Larsen sat on her chair cross-legged.

"I guess they put me here 'cause I'm a loser, huh?" said James, who wondered if all his teachers had been told he had run away.

"What kind of crazy idea is that?" Mrs. Larsen said. "I've seen your grades from Oregon. Besides," she smiled at him, "you *look* pretty sharp."

"So do you!" blurted James.

She laughed. She was wearing lots of rings and silver bracelets which jangled together when she moved her hands.

"James, this room is not a place to stick losers. It's for people who are perfectly bright but have fallen behind. Now tell me—what was your favorite course in Oregon?"

James settled back in his chair. He was beginning to feel better. "Well, we had this history course where we studied World War II. . . ."

"See," said Mrs. Larsen, pointing, jingling bracelets, "you're way ahead of us. Our sophomores are only up to the Boston Tea Party."

"No kidding," said James, leaning his elbow on the arm of the chair and gazing into her eyes, which he found quite brown and deep behind the glasses.

He still had no friends at school. The resolve that had finally brought him home was still not enough to get him through the lonely hours of classes where everyone knew everyone and nobody made an effort to know him.

He overheard two guys talking about swimming team tryouts that afternoon and decided to go. Out of 1,242 kids, nobody would care if James Hunter made the team except one very important person: himself. And that, he realized, was enough.

"He trailed the two guys on the "T" and this time he did not get lost. As he followed them up the steps of the gym he felt that old belly-tightening anticipation. It was good to be back in a locker room, smell the chlorine, feel the cold tiled floor beneath his feet. He came out of the lockers wearing his Oregon team trunks, a dry towel around his neck, feeling here, at last, he was on home turf.

"Hey," he called to some guys fooling around in the water, "where's the Coach?"

"Over there." The kid pointed across the pool. "The one yelling."

The Coach turned out to be the only person in the school who even knew he was alive—Mrs. Larsen, wearing a black tanksuit, holding a stopwatch in one hand, a megaphone to her mouth with the other, urging swimmers on just like James's old Coach in Oregon.

"Move you herd of turtles, move! Randy, get the lead out. Steve, hit those turns. Move it!"

James stared. "Mrs. Larsen . . . *Coach* Mrs. Larsen . . ."

He walked toward her in a trance. His old friends Tom and Dick were sitting in the bleachers, fully dressed. They must have come to watch a friend try out for the team.

"You finally going to get wet?" said Dick.

"Maybe he'll set a record for staying underwater," said Tom.

James continued to walk around the side of the pool to the Coach.

"Well, James," she said matter-of-factly, as if she had been expecting him all along, "we're going to run some time trials for the hundred. Think you're up to it?"

"I'm a little out of shape," he said, "but I'll try."

Mrs. Larsen blew a whistle. It echoed shrilly off the tiled walls of the pool.

"Okay, knock off," she told the kids in the pool. "Let's get some bodies over here. One-hundred time trials. Move it. Let's go. This is practice."

The kids in the bleachers quieted down. About a hundred of them had come to watch. Swimming seemed to be a bigger sport in this school than it was in Oregon.

The boys moved toward their starting positions.

"James," she said, "lane three."

He threw off the towel and stepped up.

"Swimmers are you ready?"

They mounted the platforms.

"Swimmers to your marks."

They wrapped their toes around the edge. James took a big breath of air and let it out slowly. He did it again. He looked across the pool.

Mrs. Larsen raised the whistle.

James tried to relax.

The whistle blew. He exhaled, springing off in a dive, stretching arms before him, hitting the water in a flat strong glide.

He had a lead. Hit a perfect flip turn. Mrs. Larsen looked at her watch and smiled. The guys in the bleachers were watching. They began to climb down toward the pool.

James pulled ahead. His arms were going like windmills. All he saw was unbroken green water. All he wanted was to hit that wall. He made another perfect turn.

He was on his third lap and the guys near the pool had begun to shout, "Go! Go! Go!" One of them was kneeling at the end of his lane, calling the turn for him, "*Hit it!*" and he did, catapulting halfway across the last lap of the race as the rest of the swimmers were just puffing into their turns.

His hand slapped the top edge of the pool where Mrs. Larsen was kneeling down with her stopwatch. Panting, he heard her say, "That's an unofficial record. James, you're a winner!"

He imagined the pool was draped with Olympic flags. A respectful crowd filled the bleachers. He saw himself stepping up to the winner's block with a gold Olympic medal on a ribbon around his neck. The International Olympic Band played "The Star Spangled Banner" and the sportscaster narrated, "And now ladies and gentlemen, the spectacular American champ will say a few words to our worldwide audience via Telstar."

He spoke into a microphone which was lowered from the ceiling, a hot white spotlight on his face.

"First, I would like to express my sympathy to the nations and families of those who drowned in an effort to pass me in this final race. I am sorry they cannot be standing here with me on this pedestal as they should be to share this honor. Next, I would like to thank my Coach, Marylou Larsen . . . "

And he saw her stepping into the spotlight with him, wearing a dazzling sequined tanksuit, speaking into the mike, "I have an announcement of my own. My husband, understanding and respecting my personal feelings, has granted me a no-fault divorce. James is not at fault either. It was simply meant to be. I can now become Mrs. James Hunter."

They kissed, his cold water-wet lips on her dry warm ones. The lights went on, horns blared, International confetti fell on the victorious swimmer . . .

James was pulled from his solitary fantasy by a

dozen hands. He was being lifted straight out of the water by the guys who had seen his performance from the bleachers, who suddenly didn't care if he was new or where he was from. They saw him as he really was—James Hunter, a winner. He'd made it.

And in the manner of welcoming a new member of the team, they were unanimously raising him right out of the pool—to fling him high in the air and backwards into the water, in a sprawling, laughing arc of victory.

Dell Bestsellers

- ☐ MAGIC by William Goldman $1.95 (15141-4)
- ☐ THE USERS by Joyce Haber $2.25 (19264-1)
- ☐ THE OTHER SIDE OF MIDNIGHT
  by Sidney Sheldon $1.95 (16067-7)
- ☐ THE HITE REPORT by Shere Hite $2.75 (13690-3)
- ☐ THE BOYS FROM BRAZIL by Ira Levin $2.25 (10760-1)
- ☐ GRAHAM: A DAY IN BILLY'S LIFE
  by Gerald S. Strober $1.95 (12870-6)
- ☐ THE GEMINI CONTENDERS by Robert Ludlum $2.25 (12859-5)
- ☐ SURGEON UNDER THE KNIFE
  by William A. Nolen, M.D. $1.95 (18388-X)
- ☐ LOVE'S WILDEST FIRES by Christina Savage . $1.95 (12895-1)
- ☐ SUFFER THE CHILDREN by John Saul $1.95 (18293-X)
- ☐ THE RHINEMANN EXCHANGE
  by Robert Ludlum $1.95 (15079-5)
- ☐ SLIDE by Gerald A. Browne $1.95 (17701-4)
- ☐ RICH FRIENDS by Jacqueline Briskin $1.95 (17380-9)
- ☐ MARATHON MAN by William Goldman ... $1.95 (15502-9)
- ☐ THRILL by Barbara Petty $1.95 (15295-X)
- ☐ THE LONG DARK NIGHT by Joseph Hayes . $1.95 (14824-3)
- ☐ IT CHANGED MY LIFE by Betty Friedan ... $2.25 (13936-8)
- ☐ THE NINTH MAN by John Lee $1.95 (16425-7)
- ☐ THE CHOIRBOYS by Joseph Wambaugh ... $2.25 (11188-9)
- ☐ SHOGUN by James Clavell $2.75 (17800-2)
- ☐ NAKOA'S WOMAN by Gayle Rogers $1.95 (17568-2)
- ☐ FOR US THE LIVING by Antonia Van Loon . $1.95 (12673-8)

At your local bookstore or use this handy coupon for ordering:

DELL BOOKS
P.O. BOX 1000, PINEBROOK, N.J. 07058

Please send me the books I have checked above. I am enclosing $_____
(please add 35¢ per copy to cover postage and handling). Send check or money
order—no cash or C.O.D.'s. Please allow up to 8 weeks for shipment.

Mr/Mrs/Miss_____

Address_____

City_____ State/Zip_____